"I am not here for your pleasure."

"Aren't you?" Valenti put down his knife and fork and challenged her with his full attention. It sent a shiver down her spine, and she suddenly felt conscious of the thin layer of fabric between her breasts and the cool air of the restaurant.

"No. I am not." Faye concentrated on sipping her mineral water. "I am here because, before you rudely cut short our business meeting this afternoon, you suggested you had something worth saying."

"Ahh." His pause was arrogant, his eyelids low. "So *you* prefer to digest an idea *before* your food. Very well. I *am* willing to take a chance and transfer a small advance to your business account now."

"You are?" Faye was so shocked that she almost knocked over her glass. But he had refused point-blank earlier. This made no sense. He hadn't even looked at her proposal.

"On one condition," he continued, his eyes glittering in challenge. "For the next month you will take up where you left off six years ago."

Dear Reader,

Harlequin Presents® is all about passion, power and seduction—along with oodles of wealth and abundant glamour. This is the series of the rich and the superrich. Private jets, luxury cars, international settings that range from the wildly exotic to the bright lights of the big city! We want to whisk you away every month to the far corners of the globe and allow you to escape to and indulge in a unique world of unforgettable men and passionate romances. There is only one Harlequin Presents®. And we promise you the world....

As if this weren't enough, there's more! More of what you love every month. Two weeks after the Presents® titles hit the shelves, four Presents® EXTRA titles go on sale! Presents® EXTRA is selected especially for you—your favorite authors and much-loved themes have been handpicked to create exclusive collections for your reading pleasure. Now there are more excuses to indulge! Each month there's a new collection to treasure—you won't want to miss out.

Harlequin Presents®—still the original and the best!

Best wishes,

The Editors

Sabrina Philips

VALENTI'S ONE-MONTH MISTRESS

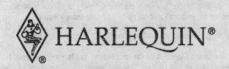

HARLEQUIN®

TORONTO • NEW YORK • LONDON
AMSTERDAM • PARIS • SYDNEY • HAMBURG
STOCKHOLM • ATHENS • TOKYO • MILAN • MADRID
PRAGUE • WARSAW • BUDAPEST • AUCKLAND

Recycling programs
for this product may
not exist in your area.

ISBN-13: 978-0-373-12808-2
ISBN-10:   0-373-12808-8

VALENTI'S ONE-MONTH MISTRESS

First North American Publication 2009.

Printed in U.S.A.

All about the author...
Sabrina Philips

SABRINA PHILIPS discovered Harlequin one Saturday afternoon in her early teens at her first job in a charity shop. Sorting through a stack of preloved books, she came across a cover featuring a glamorous heroine and a tall, dark, handsome hero. She started reading under the counter that instant—and has never looked back!

A lover of both reading and writing, Sabrina went on to study English with classical studies at Reading University. She adores all literature, but finds there's nothing else *quite* like the indulgent thrill of a romance novel.

After graduating, Sabrina began to write in her spare time, but it wasn't until she attended a course run by author Sharon Kendrick in a pink castle in Scotland that she realized if she wanted to be published badly enough, she had to *make* time. She wrote anywhere and everywhere and thankfully, it all paid off! She is absolutely delighted to have become a published author and to have the opportunity to create infuriatingly sexy heroes of her own, whom she defies both her heroines—and her readers—to resist!

Sabrina lives with her husband, who first swept her off her feet when they were both sixteen and poring over a copy of *Much Ado About Nothing*. She loves traveling to exotic destinations and spending time with her family. When she isn't writing or doing one of the above, she works as a deputy registrar of civil marriages, which she describes as a fantastic source of romantic inspiration and a great deal of fun.

For more information, please visit www.sabrinaphilips.com.

To Mum, for your unquestioning support, always.

And to Phil, for exceeding every dream
I ever had.

CHAPTER ONE

WOULD she look him in the eye and plead? he wondered. Or would she be reluctant to meet his gaze, knowing that the last time she'd held it she'd had her legs wrapped around him and had given herself to him so freely? Dante spread the report across his expansive mahogany desk and his mouth hardened. No, he doubted that. Reluctance was not a word to be associated with Faye Matteson.

Leaning back in the wide leather chair, he glanced at her name amongst the appointments in his electronic diary. When his PA had come to him last month, asking if he would agree to see her, he had immediately deduced what it was that she wanted. He knew only something like this would bring her back to Rome. But she needn't have bothered making the trip. *How* she stated her case would make no difference. He smiled wryly. It amused him that she actually believed he might be willing to help her. Like hell he would. But then why would she consider any outcome other than the one that *she* wanted? She never had before. He doubted six years had changed her. Yet it had changed him. The once angelic English waitress with the come-to-bed eyes no longer posed a danger. This time he knew she was a witch.

'Miss Matteson is here, Mr Valenti,' his receptionist purred over the intercom, interrupting his thoughts.

Dante stood up, preparing to savour the revenge.

'Send her in.'

Nothing had changed, then, Faye thought to herself as she took a deep breath and sank down tentatively on the pristine sofa indicated by the svelte redhead—the final obstacle between herself and his office. His empire might have grown, but the set-up was the same: employees still orbited around him and every woman gravitated in his direction like flowers towards the sun. No doubt he still plucked whoever took his fancy and then left them to wilt.

Faye shuddered and tried to relax her shoulders. The tension was only partly due to the after-effects of the cramped seating on last night's flight. Now was not the time to dwell on *back then*. She looked around the luxurious reception area. This world—his world—was unfamiliar to her now. Had she ever really been a part of it? She suspected that was just another delusion. There was no point even wondering. She had not *stayed* a part of it. After all these years she doubted he even recalled her name. But then it had dawned on her during the metro journey here that Dante Valenti did not allow his PA to make appointments for anyone he had not fully vetted first. So he must remember, and he had agreed for her to come anyway. Which meant… What did it mean? That the past was nothing to him, she supposed, and that business came first. *And business is all that matters now*, she berated herself silently. *It's about time you started thinking the same way*. The fact that he had agreed to see her surely meant there was a chance that he at least might be willing to help, didn't it? And there was no way she was going to blow Matteson's last hope by dwelling on a stupid, childish disappointment.

Faye checked her watch for the third time, catching sight of her freshly manicured nails, so alien to her, clutching the proposal. This had to work. It *had* to. She watched the immaculate redhead murmur into the intercom, feeling self-conscious, and swept a tendril of her own fair hair back into the clip which held it away from her face. Her budget had not stretched to a professional cut too. This would have to do.

'Mr Valenti will see you now.' The woman spoke as if bestowing upon her an undeserved honour, and ushered her towards the elaborately panelled door.

Faye smoothed down the skirt of her new grey suit unnecessarily, her heart racing, the pressure echoing at her temples. She had spent over six years believing she would never have to lay eyes on him again, and now she had brought it upon herself. But what choice did she have? Over the course of the last year she had appealed to every bank, every possible investor she could think of, but no one would lend her a penny. At first it had been disheartening, worrying. Now it was desperate. There *was* no other choice—because it was this or watch her family's restaurant go bankrupt before her eyes. And that wasn't an option. Not just because she felt instinctively that it was her daughterly duty to prevent that happening, but because *she* loved the business. So much so that she was sure even if she had been born into an entirely different family she would always have been drawn—like a bird to the south—to the simple yet deep pleasure which came from seeing other people sit together around *her* table, enjoying good food. The way people once had at every table in Matteson's. Which was why there was nothing left to do but to walk, as confidently as she could feign, into the enormous room.

He did not speak at first. Faye was silently grateful. For, though she had only dared flick a glance in his direction, the action had rendered *her* speechless. She had prepared herself for facing the old Dante, and that had been painful enough. What she had not taken into account was how time would have changed him. It was not the plush new office—he had always exuded wealth and class—nor the atmosphere of power that seemed to emanate from the ground where he stood. No, the years had somehow refined *him*. His luxurious dark hair seemed thicker, the irresistible slant of his jaw more chiselled, the curve of his full lower lip even more sensual. And those dark eyes, thrown into relief by that smooth olive skin, were the most changed of all: more piercing, more commanding— like ice. And, formidable though he looked, he was still the sexiest man she had ever met, and her treacherous eyes wanted to drink in every inch of him. Her memories had been distorted in so many respects, but she had never been wrong about that. No matter how much she wished that she had been.

'To what do I owe this unexpected pleasure, Ms Matteson?' His cut-glass enunciation of the English language with its seductive Italian undertone was as impressive to her now as it had been at eighteen, and sent long-dormant senses into overdrive. 'I can only *imagine*.'

She raised her head tentatively, not able to focus her eyes above his broad chest. He gestured brusquely for her to sit on one of the black leather chairs flanking the enormous desk whilst he remained standing, making him seem even taller than the city buildings outside the window. She perched on the edge of the chair. She wished he'd remained silent, for she had not predicted the arousing effect *that* voice would have on her in spite of the damning intention of his words. She felt the blood course faster around her veins, making her aware of pulse-points even her unrelenting nerves had not discovered.

'Hello, Dante.'

'No formalities, Faye? You need not have booked this appointment through my PA if this is, after all, a personal call.'

Faye had been more than relieved last month, when she had been able to arrange this meeting without actually speaking to Dante himself. Now she suspected this whole charade would have been easier over the phone. She had mistakenly presumed she could be more persuasive face to face, but she had she failed to anticipate the sway his physical presence seemed to have over her.

'Very well, Mr Valenti,' she said, mimicking his formal address though her throat was dry and constricted. 'I have come because I have a business proposition for you.'

'Really, Faye?' he counteracted. 'And what could you possibly have that would interest me?'

The colour rose in her cheeks and she felt utterly exposed—all the more so because of his hawk-like advantage over her. She could feel the intensity of his gaze burning through the fabric of her suit and she wanted to take off her jacket—but she didn't dare remove the layer of protection for fear that her cami would reveal the tingling buds of her breasts that thrust against the thin fabric against her will. *Straight on with the speech*, a voice inside her prompted. *Don't let him see he's getting to you.*

'My family and I are keen to find some additional investment for Matteson's, in return for a percentage of the profits. As someone who once showed an interest in our restaurant,

I thought you might be eager to see the proposal.' Her voice
trailed off as she remembered his presence there back then:
the delight that his approval had given her parents, the life he
had breathed into it for her. She opened her folder on the desk
and pushed it towards where he was standing at the other end.
He ignored the papers.

'Eager?' She did not need to look at his face to catch his
sardonic tone. 'You may have been fool enough to presume
I had any interest whatsoever in *the restaurant* back then.'
Dante dipped his eyes as he spoke, shaking his head. 'But you
must be plain stupid if you think I don't know that Matteson's
is on its last legs.'

Faye stiffened, wondering if there was anything he could
have said that would have hurt more. So it had all been a
facade. He had seen the opportunity to use *her*, nothing more.
And if he believed Matteson's was irrecoverable, she might
as well give up here and now. The thought spurred her onto
the defensive. 'Much as it might please you to believe me to
be *plain stupid*, Dante, for your information Matteson's is not
on its last legs. I admit we need an injection of cash to continue updating some elements, but—'

'An injection of cash?' Dante cut in. 'You need a miracle.
Who in their right mind is going to pump money into a business running at a loss?'

'We are *not* running at a loss.'

'But let me guess—you are not making a profit either?'

The shocking accuracy of Dante's judgement caused her
cheeks to burn, and the air in the room was suddenly stifling.
When her father had fallen ill, he had been unable to devote
the time that Matteson's demanded, and yet he had been too
proud to seek extra help, too stubborn to allow Faye to pull

out of university and share the responsibility. Faye swallowed down a lump in her throat; she admired her father for that as much as she regretted his obstinacy. But since his death things had gone from bad to worse. No matter how hard Faye had tried to turn things around profits had continued to fall, and if they didn't increase soon she wouldn't even be able to afford to pay the staff their wages.

'Perhaps if you had gained a little more experience before taking on this venture, you might not have found yourself in this position, *si*?'

The insinuation hurt. *He* was exactly the reason the broadening of her experience had been cut short. 'I have had experience. Just because it wasn't all under your guidance it doesn't mean it wasn't worthwhile. There *are* hotels and restaurants that aren't owned by you. Or hadn't you noticed?'

'I do not doubt you have had plenty of other experience since then,' Dante said slowly, deliberately running his eyes over her figure. 'But clearly none of it was quite good enough, since here you are standing before me. And we both know that means you must be desperate.'

Faye ignored the insult. He might be right about the last part, but he would mock her all the more if he knew how wrong he was about what else he was implying.

'Every business needs capital spent on it periodically. Circumstances dictate that Matteson's needs to look for an external investor now, for the first time in fifteen years. I don't consider that a failure.'

'Then open your eyes.' She recognised the harsh professional side of him she had once respected, but had never thought she would find directed at her. 'You didn't need cash back then because Matteson's was current, contemporary.

Now it's fallen so far behind it's dropped off the radar. People need change.'

Was that his personal motto? Faye wondered bitterly. And did he really suppose she was so dense that she didn't know that? She *had* tried her utmost to keep the place up to date, to turn things around after her father had passed away. But there was only so far she could get using a home printer to modernise the menus, or spending her own paltry savings on paint for the walls. She knew Matteson's needed a complete overhaul, and was desperate to give it one, but to do so she needed the means.

'It is our intention to use any funding to update the kitchens, the interior—'

'It's too late.' Dante's voice seemed to echo every rejection ever thrust her way. 'Matteson's is a failing brand.'

'Then we must agree to disagree.'

Faye raised her head, and her eyes met his for just a second before she looked back at Rome's skyline. He did not speak, but finally moved from the window towards her, making the room behind him seem larger, brighter, but the space around her feel minute. At last he rested on the desk next to her, one immaculate charcoal-suited leg casually resting over the other.

She could see the powerful thrust of his thighs and smell the earthy, masculine scent that was so distinctly his that she was transported back to another afternoon, so different from this, altogether too painful to contemplate. But forcing the images from her mind did not help to ease the old familiar pooling in her belly. She rose, unable to stand his close proximity. She wanted to scream for him to get away from her, though they must be at least a metre apart. There was no point remaining here in this room with him, enduring his vehement loathing and torturing herself when there was no hope left that this meeting would have the outcome she had wished for. No matter that when she had forced herself to consider this failure in her mind, she had thought the saving grace would be that when she walked away she would know that the way she had felt about him back then was all down to schoolgirl infatuation. She ought to be accustomed to finding that she was wrong where he was concerned.

'In that case I will approach alternative sources of funding,' she continued. His silence was unnerving. She leaned forward to retrieve the proposal, her voice laced with false optimism. 'Thank you for sparing me a moment of your precious time.'

He did not allow her to make even one complete step in the direction of the door. Before she knew what was happening he had blocked the entire movement of her body with the powerful grasp of one large, lean hand on her small wrist. Faye caught her breath.

'Leaving again so soon?' His voice was as mocking as before, only now it was cold and devoid of all humour. Faye was paralysed. 'Yet again you have done what *you* came for, but not waited to hear what I have to say. What a surprise.' The feel of his touch set her nerves skittering, enflaming her in places beyond the small area he touched.

'You have something else to say?' Her eyes were questioning, and suddenly she was the Faye of six years ago, her heart longing for some explanation to undo all the pain.

'The location *is* excellent.'

Dante released his grip on her wrist and moved back to lean against the desk. His words were like a fog and she searched within them for some hidden meaning, rooted to the spot despite the absence of his grasp.

'Wh…what?'

'You have not asked me outright whether I am interested in any aspect of your proposal—another business *faux pas*, you understand. As you rightly interpreted, I have no interest in funding Matteson's. There is, however, something that I do find extremely desirable.' Faye's head was reeling. 'The restaurant is in an exceptional location. It is in an outskirt of London I have been hoping to expand in for some time. I might consider buying the *site* for a very reasonable sum of money, if that is on offer.'

Swivelling round to face him, she felt things begin to fall into place in her mind. So *that* was why he had agreed to see her. She swallowed hard. It was his intention to finish her off completely, to usurp her family business with another Michelin-starred Valenti enterprise like the one in central London that she had taken pains to avoid for the last six years—not that she could afford to do anything but walk past. Hadn't he conquered enough already?

'Over my dead body. It is not for sale.'

'Not yet, perhaps.' He was smiling now, and it infuriated her. 'But I'll wait.'

'What do you mean by that?'

'Ahh—of course. How could I forget that waiting is a virtue that so eludes you, Faye? What I mean is I'm guessing it won't be long before it *is* for sale.'

Faye felt the colour rise hotly in her cheeks, as much at the accusation of loose morals he had just made as at the realisation of just how much he knew. For Dante was not the kind of man who *guessed* anything. He hadn't become a billionaire by burying his head in the sand. He clearly knew more about the financial state of Matteson's than she had originally thought, and it wasn't because of any distant interest he might have had in the restaurant, or in her. It was because he had seen an opportunity for himself. The thought was like a waterfall of ice down her spine. So now, if their profits failed to increase, Matteson's wouldn't just slowly fade away. He would be there to launch his brutal takeover attack.

'Well, it looks like I'll have to try my powers of persuasion elsewhere, doesn't it?' she retorted, raising her eyebrows and flashing him a smile right back. She would not let him have the satisfaction of thinking this was a *fait accompli*. So what if he had been her last possible resort? There was no harm in calling his bluff. Faye saw the wave of anger that momentarily crossed his face disappear as quickly as it had come. She suspected it was a rare thing for a woman to refuse him whatever it was he had set out to get.

'Perhaps we can come to some arrangement,' he ground out.

'Meaning what, exactly?'

'A compromise, of sorts.'

Faye doubted he knew the meaning of the word.

Suddenly the intercom in the middle of the room burst into life. 'I am sorry to interrupt you, Mr Valenti, but Mr Castillo from the Madrid office is on the line, and he says it's urgent.'

Dante swooped down to the device on the desk. 'Thank you, Julietta. Please ask him if he would be so kind as to hold for just a few minutes. I am almost finished here.'

'Of course.' The woman's voice was silky, reverent. As hers must have once been, Faye thought wretchedly. She could not help shuddering at the seductive way in which he had spoken the woman's name in return, the compassionate response that suggested he was actually something other than a cold, calculating bastard. Something like jealousy coursed through her veins, and she hated herself for it.

'Where are you staying?'

'Sorry?' His question caught her unawares.

'In Rome—where are you staying?'

'At a guesthouse near the airport. Not that it's any concern of yours.'

'No, you're not. I will have someone collect your bags, and my driver will take you to Il Maia.'

Il Maia? What was he talking about? She had never wanted to see Rome again, let alone his hotel. Now he had made it clear he had no intention of helping her, she planned to catch the next flight home. 'Even if I could afford to stay at Il Maia, it won't be necessary. I fly home tonight.'

His voice was dangerously low. 'No, you won't, Faye. Unless you want to sit back and watch the remains of your family's business crumble around you. I am willing to reconsider your proposal—on *my* terms. I will be in the hotel bar at eight, and we will discuss this over dinner.' He spoke matter-of-factly, as if the prospect could not be more unappealing. 'Since I recall that you never fulfilled the duration of your previous stay, I will kindly overlook the cost.' He motioned towards the door. 'I have more pressing business now. Julietta will show you out.'

'I am not agreeing to this when all you've told me so far is that you wouldn't touch my proposal with a bargepole!' she exclaimed, incensed by both the idea of returning to Il Maia and the prospect of spending an entire evening in his company. For one thing, she hated the thought that she might feel indebted to him, and for another, the emotions he had evoked in her during this short meeting alone quite frankly terrified her. But he was already on the intercom, telling Julietta to arrange a driver, and to put through the call from Madrid.

'Give me one good reason why I should consent to your

ridiculous proposition!' she fired out helplessly, her eyes burning with defiance.

Dante took a deep breath and turned to face her, shaking his head patronisingly. 'Because your consent is not a requirement, Miss Matteson. You will do what I tell you because I am going to make you an offer that you can't refuse, and because if you don't I'll ruin you.'

And with that he switched into perfect Spanish, and continued with his call.

Dante replaced the phone in its receiver, having rectified Castillo's supplier crisis without issue. Faye had stormed from the room the instant he'd turned his attention away from her, exactly as he'd anticipated. It was not the first time a woman had left his office sulking when things had not gone her way, and he doubted it would be the last. And yet, as he glanced at the chair where she had been sitting, he had to admit that he had been wrong about one thing. She had practically refrained from looking him in the eye for the entire meeting. The only time she had met his gaze had been when she was being bloody defiant about the dire financial state of her restaurant, and then she had looked away again just as quickly. It frustrated the hell out of him. Did she think she could fool him all over again with that feigned look of modesty?

But she had been innocent last time, hadn't she? a voice piped up in the back of his mind. It was accompanied by something else that felt disturbingly like guilt but which he refused to give any such name to. For her apparently artless innocence—which had to have been the trigger for the uncontrollable attraction she had once awakened in him—had lasted all of about five minutes! Yes, she had soon proved just how keen she was to rid herself of the *burden* of her virginity before moving on to her next victim. How long had it been? Two weeks after she had gone before she was swapping sexual favours on the other side of the Atlantic?

But God, she was just as tempting now—if not even more so. Once was not enough. Despite her coming to him begging for his money in clothes he knew she could not afford—no wonder Matteson's had reached rock bottom!—with her fingers artificially manicured when everything about her had used to be so natural, he still wanted her. It surprised him. He had felt it as soon as she had entered his office. Just like the moment he had looked up from the menu at Matteson's all those years ago to find a girl unlike any other looking back. A shy and talented young English waitress with hair like honey and legs to die for he had forbidden himself to touch. Her innocence had proved to be as false as those nails, but she still turned him on.

Saying no, telling her that the closest she was going to get to what she wanted would be watching him buy the land from under her, was not going to be enough. He needed *her* under him again. He would make her gaze into his eyes and cry out his name in pleasure, powerless to look away. Even if it did mean changing his plans a little. The end result would be the same: she would be forced to sell everything to him, to realise that if only she had been capable of a little restraint she might have been a success. He had once thought her to be unique, deserving of his respect, and he had given her the opportunity to learn from him. But she had proved that she was the same as every other woman who had tried to sink her claws into him. And now she wanted his help? Well, she had made her bed, and he was going to make damn sure she lay in it, whenever and however he chose.

CHAPTER TWO

FAYE slammed the door as soon as the hotel porter was out of sight, and flung her suitcase onto the bed. She could not remember another time in her life when she had felt her independence so utterly undermined. Yet what choice did she have but to acquiesce? She couldn't go home knowing that Dante might have considered a compromise that would stop the family business from going bankrupt and her own dreams from being torn to shreds—that rather than sacrifice her pride and go along with his egotistical demands she had decided to fly home instead of hearing him out. How could she?

It was just dinner, she supposed. When it came down to it, she had nothing to lose. If he offered her some ridiculously small sum of money for Matteson's she would simply refuse again, then get a taxi back here and head straight to the airport, knowing she had done everything she could.

Therefore, forty minutes earlier, Faye had begrudgingly followed his assistant to a car, exactly as he had instructed. Thankfully she had managed to persuade the driver to stop at the guesthouse so she could at least gather her own things on the way, rather than have someone else collect her luggage as Dante had suggested. And now here she was, back at Il Maia.

It was a very different arrival from that scorching hot July day when she had first set foot here, just over six years ago. That day her life had never felt so full of promise. Six weeks before she had been working at her parents' restaurant, waiting tables, when the most alarmingly attractive man she had ever laid her eyes upon had strolled in with such self-possession she had felt as if she was part of a film set and the star of the movie had just walked in.

'Catch of the day,' one of the other waitresses had said, and winked at her, following her line of sight.

Faye had blushed and turned away, but despite being far from alone in her awareness of him she had suddenly found herself to be the only waitress not attending to a customer. Clasping the pen and pad to her chest like a schoolgirl hugging her books, she had tentatively approached him.

'What can I get you, sir?'

He paused for a long moment, his head down.

'Whoever is responsible for this,' he said, tapping the menu with what looked to be utter disgust.

Faye froze, convinced that he was about to launch into a heated complaint. She cursed her chances for being the one to bear the brunt of it.

'Our chef is responsible for the choice of dishes on offer, sir. If there is something in particular you'd like…' Faye smiled as placidly as she could and took a step back towards the kitchen, in a gesture she hoped suggested it would be no trouble to ask.

'Not the food,' he ground out. 'The person who is responsible for this design.'

Faye felt the liquid pink that had slowly begun to drain from her cheeks rising with a vengeance.

'Actually, I am,' she said, hoping she didn't look as small as she felt.

'You?' His tone was disbelieving as he raised his head to study her face, but for one long, earth-shattering moment his eyes seemed to look deep into her soul with a burning intensity unlike anything she had ever experienced before. He shook his head and continued, 'You have this incredible talent, yet you are *waiting tables*?'

Faye was too taken aback to notice the censure in his voice, for it was then that he invited her to sit and Faye explained everything. That this was her father's restaurant and she was working there temporarily, whilst awaiting her A-level results, and that she had a passion for the whole business of hosting which came second only to her love of designing things. And that was why, whilst she was debating going to university or trying to get a job in marketing, this summer her father had finally let her loose on his menus.

When he had finished asking her every question imaginable, she realised she was beaming all over her face. It felt as if she had been invisible her whole life and that he had just bathed her in sunshine and seen her for who she really was.

'My staff, who have had years of training,' he said, lost for a moment in his admiration for her enthusiasm and talent, 'are incapable of producing something even half this original.'

And that was the moment her life had changed for ever. For in response to her wide-eyed amazement, he had announced that he was the owner of the most successful new restaurant and hotel in Rome, and that there was no way he was leaving this restaurant until she agreed to become part of his team.

It had felt as if she had just won first prize in a competition she'd never even known she had entered. Out of nowhere had come this man, as far from boys her own age as wine was from water, well-dressed, exotically Italian, with a charisma that held her in its thrall, who had created the best there was in the industry she loved. And he'd wanted *her* to work for him.

Faye remembered the feeling of pure excitement, the sensation of having arrived in every sense of the word when she had waved goodbye to her proud parents and then arrived at Rome International Airport, to find him waiting for her in his bright red sports car to personally oversee her safe arrival. But she had fallen under his spell even before that. For he could have arrived on a moped and revealed that he was actually a pizza delivery boy and she would have been just as captivated. But he *had* been everything he had said he was—and more besides. Just as the hotel had been beyond her wildest imagination—Il Maia: goddess of growth, indeed. Here, she had not only been introduced to the glamorous world of five-star hospitality, she had also lost her innocence and her heart.

Yes, this arrival at Il Maia was a very different one. Rather than being filled with a sense of freedom and anticipation, now she felt trapped here, because it was the only hope she had. But if being forced to relive the desolation of six years ago meant there was even a small chance of saving Matteson's, she was just going to have to face it.

Filled with a grim determination, Faye opened her suitcase and began hanging what few outfits she had brought with her in the enormous wardrobes along one side of the room. She sighed. She had not packed with *any* kind of dining in mind, let alone dining at one of Dante's exclusive restaurants. Eating out was, ironically, a rare thing for her these days. Though she occasionally went out for a drink with some of the girls from the restaurant when she could, it had been a long time since she had been out on this scale—and longer since she had agreed to a date. Not that this was a date, she reflected, pushing something like regret to the back of her mind.

She held up the only dress she had brought with her. It was a high-street fern-green wrap-over number that was rather too short, but she had brought it knowing the temperature here in September could still be stifling during the day. It was her only option. So what if he wouldn't consider it appropriate? He could hardly have expected her to have planned for tonight. She had spent the last of her savings on her suit for the meeting, stupidly thinking she could fool him into believing that the restaurant just needed a little extra cash to expand its already adequate profits. But now she knew he was only too aware of their dire financial situation there was no point pretending.

Faye looked in the mirror and unclipped her hair, fanning its honey-coloured length over her shoulders. In two and a half hours' time he would be downstairs, waiting for her. A frisson of anticipation shot through her. *Stupid girl*, her reflection seemed to mock. So her body still wanted him? So much was different. So much of what she had believed to be real back then was not. But she had never been wrong about the level of desire he evoked within her. She had thought it was the rose-tinted glasses of nostalgia that made her remember how her body had gone into meltdown the moment he touched her, how she had longed for his hands upon her whenever he was near, but today proved that nostalgia had nothing to do with it. Even when his touch had been simply to restrain her, rather than designed to ignite her sexually, she had not wanted it to end. Or maybe that had been precisely its purpose? she speculated as she collected fresh underwear and headed for the luxurious bathroom. She'd only had to see the way Julietta eyed him so coyly to know that he had the same effect on all women. And Dante was not the sort of man who was unaware of his own appeal. It would be exactly his style to torment her with the way he made her feel for his own ends. But it was just sexual attraction, she reasoned. Though her body might be weak, she most definitely was not. Once she had naively fallen for his charms, gladly surrendered her virginity and then slipped out of his life compliantly. But she wasn't eighteen anymore. She was older, and wiser, and had absolutely no intention of surrendering anything.

Eight-twenty. He saw her the moment she entered the room. So he would not have to go up to the suite and drag her down here. Pity. To his annoyance, several other men at the bar turned on their stools and gave her the once, then twice over. No wonder, in a dress that damned short; she always had had the most fantastic pair of legs he had ever seen. He fought the urge to walk straight up to her, wrap his hands in that golden mane of hair hanging loose over her shoulders and claim her as his own with all the force of his kiss. All in good time, he thought.

He finished the remainder of his wine and stood up before she reached him. 'I trust you had no trouble finding your way here?' he mocked, eyeing the watch at her wrist and looking upwards, as if through to the floors above.

Faye did not answer him. She had had no intention of arriving on time, even if she had been ready since seven forty-five.

'Our table is ready—do not let us refrain from the pleasure any longer.' Dante motioned for Faye to walk ahead of him.

'I agree. Let's get this over with.' She felt him place one hand lightly at the small of her back and begin to guide her through the bar into the restaurant. His touch was electric. The heat of his hand spread throughout her body. She swallowed, wanting to yell at him to back off, but she was aware that eyes were upon them. No doubt wondering what the hell the head of Valenti Enterprises was doing in one of his restaurants with *her*, and not one of the usual supermodels he did more than dine with, if the tabloids were anything to go by.

Like the rest of the hotel, the Tuscan restaurant had been simply and elegantly updated, Faye acknowledged as he led her to their table, and she didn't need to be in the restaurant business to know it remained one of Italy's most celebrated.

'Please, sit.' He held out her chair for her. 'Welcome back to Perfezione.'

Faye raised her eyebrows. Perfection; she had forgotten. Along with the rest of the staff she had known the restaurant affectionately as Fez during her month here. How had the egoism of the name never struck her back then, even if he did have a point?

'I have explained to the staff that we have important matters of business to discuss this evening. They have assured me that their disturbance will be minimal.'

Faye was not sure that was necessarily a good thing. They were seated in a fairly isolated corner. The tables cleverly concealed by vines that were the restaurant's trademark. If it was possible Dante looked even more forbidding than earlier, in a dark lounge suit and a maroon shirt open at the neck that revealed a potently masculine sprinkle of dark hair.

'I trust your room is satisfactory?' His politeness was utterly unnerving.

'*Perfezione, naturalmente.*' Two could play at the butter-wouldn't-melt game.

'I should hope so. You approve of the changes?'

'It is beautiful,' she answered genuinely, thinking how contradictory it was that in her desperation to see Matteson's tables filled with people enjoying themselves once more she had forgotten to allow herself the pleasure of eating out for what must have been months—too many to count.

Dante nodded and turned his attention to the menu. Faye watched him, unable to focus on her own. She wondered if he had any involvement in deciding what was served these days. She was not sure he would have time for the kind of attention to detail that had once so impressed her now he was based in a separate office, with restaurants all over Europe. He seemed to be looking critically, his thick, black eyelashes, outrageously long for a man, shrouding his eyes. She remembered how they had felt against her cheek, and subconsciously raised her hand to touch her face.

'I recommend the seafood.' He looked up at her, mistaking her gesture for puzzlement. 'I took the liberty of ordering an accompanying wine at the bar, but if you would prefer something else I will order another.'

'The seafood will be fine, thank you.' Faye shut her menu. 'But I will pass on the wine.'

'A mistake, you realize?'

'Perhaps.' Faye did not trust herself to keep her head on anything more than mineral water.

'And the seafood will be better than fine.'

'I don't doubt it.' Faye forgot herself for a moment, her nerves making her garrulous. 'My father used to say, "To eat well, look to the plate of your host."' The memory conjured up a childhood image of her father serving up his favourite glazed chicken and rosemary dish as the whole family waited expectantly. She remembered announcing loudly at the very same moment that she wanted to do her Brownie hostess badge.

'A wise man,' Dante agreed, his voice unusually soft. 'I was sorry to hear that he is no longer with us.'

Faye was taken aback. She had not expected Dante even to know of her father's death, let alone offer his sympathy. She could bear anything but that. Much, much easier to remember that the reason he knew was because he was waiting for Matteson's to fail in the aftermath. She nodded swiftly.

'So tell me,' she said, changing the subject, 'what offer is it that you are going to make that you think I can't refuse?'

'Patience, Faye. My grandfather used to say to me, "Do not chew over an idea until you have digested your food."'

Great, thought Faye, as Dante swiftly made their order with the waiter. *He intends to keep me dangling*.

'So, tell me, what you have been up to since…we last saw each other?' he asked, his hands together in front of him, his eyes upon her, their intensity stifling.

Trying to forget you, Faye thought, forcing down the parting image of his naked body pressed to hers.

'I travelled for a year.' Her tone was polite, stilted; she did not notice the nerve working at his jaw, her head too flooded by truths she would rather not acknowledge.

I left the country indefinitely because I couldn't bear looking up at the door in the restaurant every time it opened, jumping at the phone every time it rang, hoping it was you, finding it wasn't. Funny, how her travelling always sounded like the single most important thing she had done with her life when it had been nothing but an escape. At least going to the States to do research with Chris, who couldn't have been any more different from Dante if he'd tried, had vaguely taken her mind off him. It had beaten sitting at home wondering if she would ever hear from him again. Learning not to hope had become second nature as the months had passed. A pity forgetting him altogether had not.

'And I studied marketing,' she continued without elaboration. 'I graduated just before my father passed away. After that I naturally returned to the restaurant.'

'And that is where you wish to stay?'

At the time she had never stopped to consider whether or not it was what she wanted. That hadn't come into it. All that had mattered was that her father had devoted his life to Matteson's and there was no way she would let everything he had worked for fade to black just because he was gone. But when she thought about it, despite their dire financial situation, deep within her she knew that the restaurant business was so close to her heart that it *was* where she belonged.

Faye nodded. 'In particular my passion still lies in the design side of the business, when I get the chance.' Though that was rarely, now she was practically managing the place as well as doing shifts waiting tables.

'Really?' He raised his eyebrows. 'I was rather convinced your *passion* lay elsewhere.'

Faye's face dropped immediately. She felt as if she had been foolish to let her guard down even for a second.

'*Buon appetito*. Enjoy.'

The waiter had placed the seafood in front of them, the meals an artwork in themselves. Was the service always this immediate, or did they have every dish on standby when he was in the house?

Dante lifted his fork and looked down at his plate, his face breaking into an unadulterated smile. Faye wondered if this was another deliberate attempt to turn her on, because it sure as hell was working. She forced herself to look away, emotions warring within her. *This is the man who made love to you and then walked away.*

'You're not hungry?'

She shook her head. He looked insulted as he watched her move the food around her plate. But that only frustrated her more, for she knew damned well it was as important to him as it was to her that guests enjoyed their meal—it was just one of the things about him that had once appealed so much to her. But she didn't care; she couldn't force her appetite right now if her life depended on it. Even the very act of sitting opposite him made every muscle in her body contract.

'Contrary to popular belief, a man who takes a woman out to dinner does not find it alluring to see her eat a single lettuce leaf.'

If the misogynist in him had not been apparent earlier, it had just been biding its time. 'I am not here for your pleasure.'

'Aren't you?' He put down his knife and fork and challenged her with his full attention.

It sent a shiver down her spine, and she felt suddenly conscious of the thin layer of fabric between her breasts and the cool air of the restaurant.

'No. I am not.' She concentrated on sipping her mineral water. 'I am here because, before you so rudely cut short our business meeting this afternoon, you suggested you had something worth saying.'

'Ahh.' His pause was arrogant, his eyelids low. 'So *you* prefer to digest an idea *before* your food? But patience has its rewards.'

Did it? she wondered. What good had the months of hoping he would call done for her?

Dante signalled for the waiter and spoke to him briefly in Italian.

'Very well. You came here to join my marketing team six years ago, and you made it perfectly clear that your interest in doing so was—how shall we say?—*to gain experience of a different kind.* Once you had achieved that goal, you vanished.' He trailed his finger pensively across his jaw, as if she was a rather irritating conundrum that had just fallen out of a Christmas cracker. 'And yet you presume you have the knowledge to run a successful business? Perhaps if you had stayed longer and paid a little more attention your family's restaurant would not be where it is now.'

She had heard it all now. Was he actually arrogant enough to suggest that if she had hung around it would have prevented this whole crisis? Had he actually *expected* her to stay and face the humiliation of his rejection when he had practically packed her bags for her? She shook her head in disbelief.

'But still, despite your failing in this, Matteson's is in an excellent location,' he continued.

Here we go again, she thought. *He's just trying to convince me that I'm such a failure I might as well sell now.*

'Therefore I am willing to take a chance and transfer a small advance to your business account now, with the rest of the sum you desire to follow in a month.'

'You are?' Faye was so shocked that she almost knocked over her glass. But he had refused point-blank earlier. This made no sense. He hadn't even looked at her proposal.

'On one condition,' he continued, his eyes glittering in challenge. 'For the next month, you will take up where you left off six years ago, and you will learn everything you need to make Matteson's a success. Then, and only then, will I loan

you the full sum you request. When you return home you will
have one further month to double your profits.'

Faye looked at him, wanting to see something in his expression that would suggest he was joking. It wasn't there.

'And if I fail?'

'The restaurant is mine.'

CHAPTER THREE

TAKE up where she'd left off? Her chest constricted at the thought. As Faye reeled from his ultimatum and all it spelled for Matteson's, that was the only thing her brain seemed capable of processing. Surely he didn't mean—? She shook herself. He was talking about her *work* experience. Yet even the thought of living back here at Il Maia, where she had spent the best and worst four weeks of her life, filled her with alarm. Where would that leave *her* at the end of the month? How could she see this man every day when she was torn between wanting to scratch that triumphant smile from his lips and wanting to taste them?

It seemed a foregone conclusion that she was ruined whether she accepted his ridiculous proposal or not. Doubling the turnover within such a short space of time was near impossible. Yet refusing his offer was out of the question. For if she did she'd be willing to bet he'd make sure Matteson's folded in double-quick time, just so he could pick up the pieces, work his multimillion-dollar magic and then flaunt his success in her face.

'I suppose the fact that what you expect me to achieve within a month is impossible is part of the joke?'

She watched his lean fingers with their neatly shaped nails stroking the stem of his wine glass ominously. His eyes rested threateningly upon her, as if she were his prey and the slow kill was his preference.

'I never joke about business. You asked for my help. These are my conditions.' His arrogance was almost tangible. He sat completely still. It only seemed to emphasise that, to him, this whole affair was barely worth his energy.

'This is a game to you, isn't it?'

'Life is a game.'

'People's livelihoods are at stake.'

'Then win.'

Faye leaned back in her chair, feeling the pulse throb at her temples. 'Could I not have the full sum now? Have the renovations well underway by the time I return?' She subconsciously shook her head as her mind tried to fathom some way of achieving the unachievable.

'Ahh, what a surprise. Miss Matteson is both loath to wait and unable to see that the *priceless* offer of working with me is worth more than any payout.'

'You always did have the most monumental ego.'

'And yet you have come back for more?'

Faye glowered at him.

'Silence, Faye? Just when I was growing so fond of your new spirit.'

Anger bubbled within her veins like volcanic lava, and her eyes dropped to her glass of water. She was racked with a sudden desire to see it splashed all over his smouldering features. Only the buzz of other diners made her hesitate. He second-guessed her.

'Go right ahead,' he challenged, as her eyes darted around

the room. 'You think it will hurt *my* reputation? You're the one who will be working here. I, on the other hand, am used to the childish behaviour of clients unable to control themselves when they do not get their own way.'

'And what about when *you* don't get your own way, Dante? You blackmail your *clients* until they do?' Faye rose, placing her serviette on the table.

'Blackmail?' He made it sound as if she'd just accused him of murder. 'I think you'll find I've offered you a lifeline.'

She'd hate to see him offer the opposite.

'Sit, Faye.' Could he be any more patronising? 'If you walk away, my offer is withdrawn, and the day you go under I will be there—waiting. I will offer you even less than the site is worth, and you will be forced to accept. Now, sit down.'

His tone was low and silky, and the effect it had upon the muscles in her legs would have made the decision for her even if the cold truth of his words had not. Slowly she resumed her seat, her face stony. She could not bring herself to look up at the expression of self-satisfied triumph he undoubtedly wore.

'Dessert.' She was grateful for the interruption as the waiter positioned large plates in front of them.

'Torta di Ricotta,' Dante announced.

Faye did not answer him. She could be eating ambrosia, the food of the gods, and it would still taste bitter to her.

'You imagine that Matteson's will be able to cope without me?'

'Presumably someone has been running it the last couple of days.'

Technically, Faye's mother was in charge of the restaurant in her absence, but whilst Josie Matteson was desperate to see Matteson's restored to its former glory, she had always played a supportive role. In reality the workload would be spread between the head waitress and the chef. She trusted them both, but it was far from ideal.

'Do not tell me that you, who are so critical of my ego, consider yourself indispensable, Faye? I can assure you, you are not.'

No, she doubted any woman was indispensable to Dante Valenti. How long had it been after he had walked away from her bed before he had taken another lover. Hours? Days?

'Impetuous change may be part and parcel of your hectic lifestyle, Dante, but I can assure you it is a rare thing for us lesser mortals.'

'Ah, but when there is opportunity you are only too eager?'

'Not on this occasion.'

'And how coincidental that your reluctance comes when it means not getting your cash at the click of your fingers.'

'I can assure you that my reluctance has nothing to do with your money and everything to do with you.'

'And yet you used to be so keen for both?' His voice was husky now, and Faye almost dropped the first spoonful of dessert that she had taken. 'Or has it slipped your mind that you once begged me to make love to you?'

So he was not going to let her forget it. Though she had been trying to prevent herself reliving that fateful afternoon since the moment she had arrived, he had every intention of using it against her. She sank back in her chair, feeling defeated.

It had been the first of August. Saturday. She would never forget the date. The evening before they had worked ceaselessly to meet a deadline, with Faye sketching idea after idea for the new hotel brochure. Production meetings had run late into the night. Not that Faye had noticed the unsociable working hours. She had been too exhilarated that she was a part of all this.

In fact, even during her time off she'd caught herself wishing she were back at the office, with that feeling of awareness zipping around her veins at a double-quick pace just at knowing he was close by, which quadrupled when he looked at her. And there had been many times in the course of the last four weeks, unbelievable though it was, when she had caught him doing just that. And not in the way that an employer usually looked at his employee. More in the way an art lover might examine the ceiling of the Sistine Chapel. But he would always look away the moment she noticed, his brows furrowed, as if he had really been contemplating some complex business problem and had just alighted upon the answer. Which had left Faye caught between believing she was too young and too awkward for him to see her as anything other than the teenage girl she was, and sensing something else within him that he seemed reluctant to acknowledge.

'Faye?' He had spoken her name as if coaxing a child from sleep. She'd finished off the section of the cover design she was working on and attempted to steady the pounding of her heart before looking up to see him standing before her desk.

'I'm almost done.'

'It's late.' He looked at his watch and raised his eyebrows. 'It's the weekend, and I've been working you like a Trojan. Go and get some rest.'

Faye's eyelids did indeed feel heavy. 'OK. I'll pop back tomorrow morning—get this finished before Monday.'

'No, you won't,' he said, his voice insistent. 'You deserve a break. Go out—soak up Rome at the weekend.'

Faye nodded hesitantly. She had taken herself out on a sightseeing bus tour the weekend after she had arrived, but magnificent though the sights were, seeing them by herself, without anyone to share her amazement, had somehow diminished their appeal.

'Perhaps.'

It was then that Dante looked around the room thoughtfully, at the rest of his team slowly packing up and making their ways home.

'I suppose there isn't really anyone else here your age.' His expression was guilty. 'I'm sorry.'

Faye knew it was true, although it was not something that had bothered her. Until he had pointed out how young she was again. She didn't *feel* young.

And then he said it.

'I could always show you the sights tomorrow, if you like.'

And those words changed everything.

For the Dante who was waiting for her in the lobby the next morning—a Dante without the immaculately pressed suits he wore to work—was everything she had hoped for and more besides. It felt as if somehow they were equal, like any other couple getting lost amongst the crowds. For not only did he make the sights come alive—from the wonder of Vatican City to the Baroque fountains hidden amongst the lesser-known ancient sights—he also had insisted she experience the intimate *trattorie*, the sensational boutiques in Piazza di Spagna.

She marvelled at their windows, not daring to go in. Until he called her over to one particularly exclusive display and she saw the most exquisite red evening gown she could ever have imagined. The kind most women never got to wear, let alone own.

'Go in,' he commanded, sensing her appreciation. 'Try it on.'

'Oh, Dante—don't be ridiculous. Why would I try on a dress like that? The assistants will only have to take one look at me to know that I don't have the money to even buy the hanger, let alone an occasion to wear the dress.'

'Nonsense,' he said, as if she had just suggested the earth was flat.

And the sudden understanding of just how powerful and how rich Dante really was began to seep in as she was ushered to a fitting room that was so large it could have given the entire upstairs in her parents' house a run for its money.

The dress fit like a glove, but it was with some trepidation that she stepped out, feeling like a peasant masquerading as a princess. Slowly he turned around, and then did a double-take, as if to check it was really her. She hadn't anticipated that it would be the way he looked at her rather than the dress itself that would make her feel as if her whole body was glowing. But she knew she wanted to bottle the feeling and keep it for ever.

'Faye…*bella*,' he said guardedly, his voice a purr. 'You look …' He shook his head like a man torn and turned to the shop assistant. 'We'll take it.' The woman smiled from ear to ear and waltzed off to the till.

'Dante, what are you doing?' Faye protested under her breath, trying not to move for fear she might damage the priceless gown. 'I can't afford this!'

'Think of it as a thank you for all your hard work,' he said abruptly, avoiding looking directly at her. 'Now, go and get changed.'

And, despite her protestations, Dante paid for the dress before she even emerged from the changing room.

Feeble though it was in comparison, she insisted she buy
him a *gelato* in return. Puzzled by her insistence, he reluctantly
agreed—on the condition that he take her to the best place to
sample delicious ice cream. But just as they were approaching the winding street he had in mind, the heavens opened.

By the time they had run back to Il Maia, her hand reaching
for his to stop them losing one another in the crowds of
shoppers, her light summer dress was soaked through and
stuck to her body, and his pale shirt was clinging to his broad
chest, his jeans moulded to his lean hips. Finally they reached
her room, and, breathless and laughing, she unlocked the door
and flew in.

Dante hesitated in the doorway.

'My apartment's only a few blocks away. Let me head
back and get changed. I'll meet you downstairs.'

'Dante, it's raining even more heavily now—here, have a
towel.' Faye slipped off her shoes and flitted through to the
bathroom. He stood there, poised like a man who had been
asked to do a bungee jump without a rope.

'No, Faye, I shouldn't—'

'Come on, you'll get cold.' Faye pulled him into the room,
laughing, and put the towel around his shoulders, shutting the
door behind him.

And the moment the catch clicked shut, something
snapped. The air in the room changed, and her naturally quick
movements seemed to slow as she became conscious of every
move her body made. The smell of rain mixed with her faint
floral perfume and his musky cologne. Their damp clothes
seemed to long to be removed. She was thrilled at being
caught out by nature, as if it was urging them to come together.

She stood before him, the intensity of the look he gave her

making her nipples peak beneath the wet cotton of her dress. His silence was unbearable.

'Let's get out of these clothes,' she said, reaching her arm behind her back, turning around. 'Help me with this zip.'

He did not answer, but she felt him move behind her and his hands begin to release her dress, agonisingly avoiding contact with her skin. Faye heard her breathing fall in time with his. It was as if those lingering glances had reached fever pitch and there could be no more looking away. Faye...*bella*. The words echoed around her mind, refusing to be forgotten, and her body was crying out for him as the rivulets of water ran over her body, mingling with its own heat.

'Touch me, Dante.'

She did not know where the words came from. She whispered them in a voice she did not recognise as her own—knew only that she needed him in a way she had never understood needing anything before. His warm breath stirred the hairs on the back of her neck, but still he did not move.

'Please.' She turned round to face him and looked up at him, her eyes wide, imploring. 'Please, touch me,' she urged.

Dante drew in a ragged breath, his eyes boring into her with unfathomable intensity. She saw his hands move up as if to encircle her waist, and then drop to his sides again.

'I want...' Her voice was bolder now, seeing his temptation. 'I want you to make love to me.'

'Damn you, you little temptress,' he bit out, his voice thick as he shook his head slowly. 'Don't you know what you do to me?'

She nodded slowly, her lips parted. And then he raised his head and looked deep into her eyes for one final moment, before he brought his mouth crushing upon her own.

And it was then that Faye truly learned what it was to be touched. To feel the exquisite pleasure of being claimed by the man you loved in the most intimate way there was. And the sudden searing of pain was replaced by a mounting pleasure which exploded with all the unexpected welcome of a late-afternoon storm. A sensation which, to Faye, was only surpassed by the feeling of lying beneath a cool white sheet, with Dante just inches away afterwards, and the sound of the easing rain outside the window. The sound of his breathing was steady and deep.

'Couldn't you just stay here for ever?' she whispered.

It was the eye of the storm she had never seen coming.

'I thought you had got everything you wanted.'

Faye's face crumpled. She didn't know what he was supposed to say *afterwards*, but she knew that wasn't it. Seconds before he had been crying her name in ecstasy—and now? Now the harshness of his tone made it sound as if he almost *despised* her.

Faye rolled away from him, whipping the sheet around her. 'What are you talking about?' She suddenly felt as if she was playing a complicated game and no one had told her the rules.

'I'm talking about little girls who cast all dignity aside the minute they get a taste of the high life.' He glanced towards the designer bag containing the dress and curled his lip in distaste. 'Those who are so hot for a man they do not see the value of their virtue amidst their haste to lose it.'

He swung his legs over the bed, shameless in his nakedness, and reached for his damp jeans.

'You came here to learn, *bella*? Then today you learn this is not the kind of behaviour which makes a man *stay* anywhere. Why would he, when he has taken all that is worth taking?'

And with that he scooped up the rest of his clothes and headed towards the door. Suddenly it didn't feel like a game at all.

'What are you talking about?' she repeated helplessly, searching his face, willing him to take the words back.

'Your true colours, *sì*?' he said with finality before closing the door calmly behind him.

As Faye stared helplessly at the door, nausea rising in her belly, she felt her heart break in two. Felt all the humiliation of loving so blindly, of discovering just why it all felt so unreal. Because it was. Every moment, from the instant they had met until now, turned sour in her mind, as if someone had poured acid into her brain. And something changed irrecoverably within her. Not because she had just made love to a man for the first time in her life. But because all her foolish childhood dreams had just crashed out through the door with him. She had wanted to give herself to him, and he detested her for it. How could she have got it so wrong?

Faye choked back the sobs as realisation seeped in, and suddenly she was caught by a need to get dressed—as if angry at her own body, determined to cover its nakedness. The open wardrobe caught her eye, with its skirts and blouses neatly ordered for her weeks of work ahead. Yes, she thought, there *was* something worse than this: staying around to face the humiliation day after day, having him look at her thinking he had *taken all that was worth taking*, having him look at her at all.

And so she packed her bags. Understanding that her leaving would have about as much impact on his world as a pebble skimming the surface of the ocean, but knowing it was preferable to being swallowed up by the ocean completely.

* * *

Faye raised her head to look at him, sitting opposite her, her heart numb with the steady ache she had not allowed herself to feel for so long. She felt ashamed—that she had had no choice but to swallow her pride and return, that she had allowed him to get to her once more—and she felt terrified that she was capable of letting him do it all over again.

'As you said yourself, Dante, we all make mistakes.'

He seemed oblivious to the pain in her eyes. 'You mean you realised that you could have got more for your virginity than a few weeks working here?'

What was he talking about? She had wanted nothing from him but for it to have been real. Yet *he* was angry with *her*? She looked at his cruel, arrogant, despicably handsome face. He seemed to tire of waiting for her to answer. She was glad.

'It was fortunate that you were offered *opportunities* elsewhere, in spite of having come straight from me.'

'Not everyone is such as Neanderthal as you, Dante. Some men do not consider a woman's virginity the only thing she has to offer,' she bit out, furious at his assumptions, and even more furious that she had never brought herself to take up any such *opportunities*, as he put it, on the occasions when they had come her way. But what would have been the point? She hadn't even once got close to feeling anything like she had felt that afternoon with anyone. Until she had walked into his office again today, she thought wretchedly.

'Faye, do not misinterpret me. I meant opportunities in the business world. Not many people walk out on a contract with Valenti Enterprises and are still offered work elsewhere.'

Bastard, she thought. Like hell you meant that. And as for business opportunities—those that had come her way since, she

had had to turn down for the sake of Matteson's. Faye felt all
the tension in her shoulders return as she put down her spoon.

'Champagne to finish, I think. A toast to my new…right-
hand woman for a month.'

Faye gritted her teeth. There was no reason to refuse. She
had sold her soul to the devil. If she was worried about losing
her head, it was too late.

As he chinked his glass against her own, the blood in her
veins slowed to a more languorous pace, no less insistent. She
wished she had brought her *faux* pashmina to cover herself from
that penetrating gaze which lingered upon her as she took a sip.
Did he want her? He hated her, wanted to ruin her—she knew
that. But she also knew that was not an issue he'd have diffi-
culty putting aside if he did. The bubbles fizzed on her tongue.
She took a deep breath as the alcohol reached her bloodstream,
making her more conscious of her surroundings. Two days ago
she had woken up to face a day like any other at the restaurant:
vacant tables, piles of bills, tired décor, tired people. And now
here she was, sitting in Perfezione, the antithesis of her life back
home. Surrounded by so much luxury, so much life, in a restaurant where it took months just to secure a booking. Unless
you happened to be accompanying the man who had haunted
her dreams to this day. For a moment she wondered if she had
conjured up this whole scene in her imagination.

'I will have a contract drawn up, which you can sign
tomorrow.'

No, not a dream. She nodded reluctantly. He *was* the devil
in disguise. So she had no choice but to stay, but she did not
have to stay *here*. She would return to the guesthouse. Even
if it meant having to put it on a credit card and negotiate the
busy metro every morning, she needed her escape.

'Excuse me.' Faye caught the attention of a passing waiter, ignoring Dante as he stiffened. 'Please could you order me a taxi to Piazza Indipendenza? *Grazie.*'

'That won't be necessary, Michele. I will drive Miss Matteson. Thank you,' Dante interjected, almost before she had even finished. The waiter was dismissed instantly and was so professional that not a hint of perplexity crossed his face.

'You've been drinking. You're not driving me anywhere!' Faye made no effort to tone down the volume of her anger now. She had had enough of this rollercoaster of emotions. One minute he was masquerading as a reasonable human being, and the next he was verging on the tyrannical.

'I'm glad you agree. I will not be driving you anywhere, because we have established that you will stay here—have we not?'

'I have agreed to *work* for you. Where I stay has no bearing upon that. I will make sure I am on time, if that is your concern.'

'That is not my concern, and it shall not be yours either. Living here is as much part of your experience as your work here during the day. It is not up for debate.'

No, nothing *he* decided was up for debate, was it? And no wonder, when his world was full of people pandering to his every need, treating his every word like the Holy Grail. But whilst he might get her diffident agreement, he would not have this ridiculous facade of civility any longer. She would get on with what she was here to do, and spend as little time in his company as possible.

'I wish to go to bed. I had a late flight.'

'Bed? Why, you should have said earlier.' He rose, his hand moving to her elbow and his mouth lifting into a lazy lopsided grin that was at odds with the brooding intensity she had seen on his face for most of the day.

How was he allowed to look so good when he was so damned unscrupulous? She tried not to notice. She had allowed him to trample over her youthful emotions wearing that sexy smile once before, and she was not going to let him do it again.

'I can make my own way up three flights, Dante.'

'I insist on seeing you back to your room, *bella*.' He whispered the word in her ear as they walked away from the table. *Bella*. She wondered how her legs kept moving with such tantalising remembrance flooding back.

Faye led the way up the stairs, not prepared to face the intimate space of the lift with him. She could feel him close behind her, the sounds of the foyer and the restaurant dying away as they ascended. She would never be able to escape him; she never could. Even nine hundred miles away, he had always been there in her head, making every other man appear as a mere shadow.

They came to a stop outside her room, and she fixed her eyes firmly on the thick wooden door, determined to put it between them. This close he was dynamite. She wanted—no, needed to defuse it.

'Goodnigh—'

'Look at me,' he ground out, one hand suddenly tilting her chin so that she had no choice in the matter, his other hand against the wall behind her head, trapping her. His face was so close to hers she could see the angry flaring of his nostrils and the first sign of stubble on his chiselled jaw. She fought the urge to touch it. 'You can't hide any longer.'

'I'm not trying to hide.'

'Liar.'

She looked into his eyes. Their black depths glittered with hunger, and they were her undoing. She wanted to tell him not to look at her that way. And at the same time she never wanted him to stop. She let out a sigh she was not even sure was hers, all the fight from her gone. His gaze dropped to her lips. He did want her. She could see it in the way he almost clenched his teeth in resistance as his thumb came up to touch her bottom lip invitingly.

'Dante!'

She closed her eyes, almost out of fear that if she kept them open she would awake from this moment. She did not. Half of her was convinced he would back away, whilst the other half expected him to claim her mouth in one fierce, demanding stroke. Neither. Her lips parted as if he had coaxed them subliminally at the exact moment he brought his own down to meet them, and for a second he held them there, as if they were some timeless statue, caught for ever in the most sublime moment of anticipation. And then slowly, painfully slowly, he brushed his lips against her own, gently exploring her, teasing her into deepening the kiss, beginning to taste her. His tongue found hers and slid across it, sending feelings of anticipation throughout her entire body, the movement loaded with sensual promise. Hunger enveloped her. His hand at her chin reached to tangle itself in her hair, cradling her head at the perfect angle for him to kiss her more and more deeply.

What had he done to her all those years ago that made him the only man on earth who could melt her with a single gaze? He had imprinted himself upon her very soul. But as yearning flooded her body like a drug she gave up wondering and surrendered to the urgent sensation that threatened to take her over, sliding her arms behind his broad back, crushing her breasts against his powerful chest, her whole body throbbing with need.

But in that moment she felt his lips break away from her, creating a new and unwelcome void that demanded to be filled by him alone. Yes, she thought, amidst the blur of desire in her mind. Not here. Inside. She lifted her eyelids drowsily, ready to lead him into her room. And the piercing black stare that met her own lust-filled gaze chilled her to the bone.

'You think, perhaps, that a speedy capitulation might encourage me to part with the entire sum early?' His tone was merciless. He shook his head and tutted. The arms that she had wrapped around his body fell to her sides. 'I know you are gagging for me, *cara*, but patience is one of the first rules of business. Never offer your best assets first. You have made this mistake in the past, yes? See—you learn the first lesson already. We have all month to sample dessert.'

Faye's teeth bit down on her kiss-swollen lips, hot colour staining her cheekbones, the desire that had coursed through every inch of her replaced with a humiliation equally difficult to quell. She turned away from him, wanting to knock the satisfaction from his face, but feeling a moistness in her eyes that she would rather die than have him observe.

'Forgive me,' she muttered, her voice like poison as she unlocked the door of her room, 'for assuming that conceding to your barbaric behaviour was a requirement of this deal. I obviously misunderstood. Now I know I am excused in that department, I assure you nothing will give me greater pleasure than to stay as far away from you as possible.'

Dante laughed—a loud, shameless laugh that shook her to the very core. 'I will teach you about pleasure too, *cara*, but all in good time.' Before he had even finished his sentence she had flown into the dark room and closed the door hurriedly behind her, her hands still shaking. She stood with her back to the wall, a shiver rushing over her as the cool evening breeze blew the curtain at the balcony in an ebbing and flowing motion that reminded her of an old horror film. She had never felt so utterly rejected. She held her breath, unwilling to exhale until she was sure he was gone. Finally she let out a long, deep sigh. The moment she did, his voice penetrated the thick door.

'You begin work tomorrow morning at seven-thirty, in the kitchen. Do not be late.'

CHAPTER FOUR

FAYE caught the white apron that was thrust into her hands and grudgingly tied it around her waist. Attempting to blink herself awake, she followed the petite kitchen hand who had introduced herself as Lucia to an enormous sack beside a space at one of the work surfaces. She wanted to ask precisely how peeling sweet potatoes at this time in the morning was going to help her rescue her family's business, but she held her tongue. Though she knew this was contributing to nothing more than Dante's already inflated ego, there was no reason to take it out on Lucia, who was simply another member of the army of staff that gladly catered to his every whim.

As Lucia left her to it, Faye looked around the enormous kitchen and sighed. Yet oddly, as she took in the sea of whites, stainless steel and concentrated expressions, she somehow felt impelled to prove to him that, regardless of what he thought, she was not afraid of hard work. As she knuckled down to her task the minutes soon ticked by, and she began to find the repetitive action strangely therapeutic.

She had had a restless night, caught between sleep and waking, fighting the feeling of utter rejection and the overwhelming desire to open the door just to check whether Dante was still hovering there like some elusive phantom, even though she knew he was long gone. At least the fastidiousness of the Perfezione kitchen kept her mind from wondering whether she was simply here to amuse him, even if this whole exercise was actually an extension of that.

She had almost expected him to be here this morning, if only to check that she had not gone AWOL during the night. But when she discovered that Lucia was to be responsible for her *experience*, today at least, Faye realised that in complying with his scheme she had no doubt relinquished any special treatment. Now he as good as had a free employee for the month, and when she failed in her task Matteson's would be his. Even if for some unthinkable reason she succeeded, he would get his money back and she would be gone from his life for good. From his point of view it was a win-win situation. She, on the other hand, had everything to lose, she thought as her mind wandered over the brief telephone conversation she had had with her mother that morning.

'Oh, Faye, that's wonderful news!'

Faye had tried not to inject her voice with too much optimism as she'd told her mother that she had secured enough funds to contract the first renovations, but after endless months of bills and 'application refused' letters dropping through the letterbox at the restaurant, it was no surprise that Josie Matteson had been delighted.

'It's not a simple loan, though, Mum. There are…conditions.' Faye pushed the disturbing image of Dante's *conditions* to the back of her mind. 'I'm going to have to stay here for the next month.'

Aside from telling her mother that she was going to Italy in one final bid to secure a loan, Faye had been vague about her exact plans. But she *had* said that she would only be gone a couple of days at most. If only.

'I'm sure we can cope,' her mother replied, fretful for a second. 'Yes—of course we can.'

Though Josie Matteson was as desperate as Faye to see the restaurant restored to its former glory, she had always been happier keeping the place spic and span than getting involved in the managerial side of things.

'Was last night busier?' Faye asked hopefully. If only some miracle had occurred whilst she had been away. Then she could tell Dante what to do with his contract and get back to where she was needed. But she knew she had about as much chance of having drummed up enough business with that last frantic leaflet-drop as she had of being married with a baby by the time she was twenty-five.

'It was quiet again, I'm afraid, darling. Even that anniversary booking was cancelled. Apparently they hadn't been to us for years, and when one of them popped in to see the place they changed their minds.'

Faye felt her heart sink as she envisaged another empty table. But at the same time it seemed to fill her with a renewed sense of resolve to see this whole excruciating but necessary charade through to the end. It was the only thing that offered her a chance to change all that.

'But let's not dwell on that now, when we've just had good news about this kind soul offering us a loan,' Josie continued.

Faye was grateful that her mother couldn't hear the alternative opinion of Dante running through her head, for the thought of explaining just why he was anything but a *kind soul* was too loathsome to contemplate. Nevertheless, whilst her mother wasn't one to probe, this was about Matteson's, and she at least deserved to know where the money was coming from.

'I…um…approached Valenti Enterprises,' Faye said, as if avoiding his Christian name would stop Josie making a connection with the past—though she doubted her mother had forgotten. After all, though it had been many years ago, it wasn't every day that she found her daughter over the moon at being offered the opportunity of a lifetime, only to have her return out of the blue, suddenly desperate to take up Chris's long-standing offer, with a list of excuses for leaving Italy as long her arm. That the job hadn't been what she was expecting. That the language barrier had been too difficult. That there had been no one her own age. In hindsight, Faye realised she had protested so much that it had had nothing to do with *him* that she had given herself away.

Her mother's momentary silence seemed to confirm it.

'That can't have been easy, Faye. Mr Valenti is a formidable man. But he was once impressed with what he found here. He must remember.'

Oh, he remembers, all right, thought Faye as she steered the conversation back to the practicalities of her absence. That's precisely the problem.

Several hours later, when she had finished the potatoes, Faye was surprised that Dante had arranged for her to be shown how some of the dishes on the day's lunch menu were prepared. She was delighted to find that the chef in charge was Bernardo, who had started as a junior the season that Faye had first arrived at Il Maia.

'Faye! Come. I show you risotto!'

It's lucky, she thought, that his English isn't good enough to ask me what the hell I'm doing back here.

It was amazingly inspiring, watching the staff work so harmoniously together in this high-tech set-up, and she couldn't help but admit that the experience did give her a fresh outlook. It reminded her of her own enthusiasm for serving good food, that in recent months had become buried under the stress of poor profits. For, whilst Dante's attitude to her might leave plenty to be desired, she couldn't deny his skills as a restaurateur.

Faye was laughing raucously at Bernardo's gestures as he tried to demonstrate how the mushrooms for the risotto were harvested, when she felt the air change. The doors to the kitchen had been opening and closing all morning, but somehow she knew that the person who had just entered the room was not simply any other member of staff. She stopped laughing immediately as she sensed footsteps behind her. *Dante.* For some reason she felt utterly guilty, like a small child caught with her hand in the sweet tin. Even Bernardo looked as if he wished he were not there, despite the fact he had been carrying out his boss's wishes. She turned round, knowing without looking exactly where he stood. He was wearing a jet-black suit that only enhanced the darkness of his hair, contrasting lucidly with the gleaming bright white of the kitchen. His mouth was fixed in a hard line. For a man so well-known for his control, he looked as if it might evade him for a moment.

'Good afternoon.' Faye smiled brightly, determined to counteract her unwarranted guilt. 'What can we do for you? Lunch, perhaps?' She thought she saw a nerve move at his jaw, and turned to Bernardo, grinning. 'I can recommend the mushroom risotto.' Bernardo shifted on his feet a little uneasily, and turned back to his preparations.

Dante did not seem willing to dignify her question with an

answer. Did he have to be such a brute? She supposed he would have preferred to find her elbow-deep in potato peelings, lamenting her fate.

'I see Bernardo has had plenty of time to share his expertise. If you speak to Lucia, she will see that you are organised to serve lunch for the rest of the afternoon.' He delivered his speech as if he was diagnosing a disease, and turned on his immaculate heels to head for the door without waiting for a response.

'Believe it or not,' she called after him, 'I have waited tables before. Just as I'm quite capable of preparing vegetables *and* following a recipe. Could you explain to me how this is supposed to help me increase my profits?'

The kitchen went silent, save for sound of billowing steam from a large saucepan. The other workers continued diligently, ears undoubtedly pricked. Dante swung round and closed the gap between them, so that his face was level with hers and disturbingly close. His eyes were full of challenge, as if she had dared him.

'I am going to make you fall in love,' he announced, his voice smooth and low.

Faye stood on her tiptoes, as if the extra inch was some small semblance of defence against him, and drew in a breath. She parted her lips, half in shock and half because she felt she should say or do something, without knowing what. She knew what had flashed into her brain, but there was certainly no question of doing *that*.

'With this business,' he finished nonchalantly, as if his sentence had never suggested anything else. 'With the sights, the smells, the tastes of Perfezione. I am going to make you want to give *your* customers the pleasure you will see on people's faces here, and you are going to learn how to instil that same want in your staff.' His voice assumed an acidic timbre. 'But I see you have already learned something of the wants of my staff this morning.'

Faye fell back on her heels, not following Dante's glance in the direction of Bernardo, who was now furiously working away at the stove. She was momentarily stunned, and when she raised her head to look at him again he was eyeing her as if he wished she would disappear. As the words sank in, it infuriated her that his intention had worked—for she had always loved this business, and yet she had felt more inspired this morning than she had done for years.

'You need to change,' he said casually, as he looked her up and down, before walking towards the door. It took until he was long gone for Faye to realise literally what he meant.

Dante sat down at a table by the window, tossed his jacket aside, and loosened his tie. The manipulative temptress! She had been here less than twenty-four hours and she had already found a way to pout those kissable lips and flash those bewitching green eyes to her advantage in the most assiduous kitchen in Italy. *His* kitchen. How had he ever been stupid enough not to see through her?

Unwillingly, he thought back to the day he had by chance set foot in Matteson's. He'd been in London checking out potential sites for expansion and any likely competition. He hadn't expected to find the fresh new look he wanted for his branding staring up at him from his lunch menu. But then he knew that the best things in life were never be to found where you most expected them. Recognising that had been the secret of his success. But how much easier it would have been on that occasion if the innovative design before him had been the work of some hugely expensive marketing company in some far-flung corner of the world. He could have simply bought it up and claimed it without complication.

Instead he had discovered it was the work of a waitress, a girl who was barely out of high school. A girl he had not only found irresistibly attractive, but who had evoked in him another feeling he couldn't quite lay his finger upon—and that had surprised him. Had it been because she was English? No, he had had English lovers. Because she was beautiful? Yes, she had a fresh-faced beauty women would kill for and men would die for, but it wasn't the kind that would be wholly captured by a photograph. Because a photo wouldn't have been able to capture her unaffected *joie de vivre*, or her innate enthusiasm for the business that he'd been surprised to find reminded him of his own, but without any of the cynicism that had come from his being too often surrounded by people who lacked it. He never usually looked twice at women that young or that innocent. But when had been the last time—no, when had he *ever* come into contact with a woman whose innocence he truly believed so wholeheartedly? The truth was, he had both admired and *respected* her. Which was why—the minute he'd offered her an opportunity to work with his marketing team—he had made a pact with himself never to touch her.

But, *Dio*, how she had seen an opportunity for something else entirely! So quick to rid herself of the purity that he had held in such regard that he had suppressed his own longings— which was something Dante Valenti simply didn't do. And how little she had deserved it! He remembered that fateful day, when he had seen what he should have recognised the first time she blinked those enormous earnest eyes at him. Eyes which had spoken even louder than her cries for him to take her. What man could have fought against it any longer? Dante swallowed defensively, pushing down the feeling of something like shame as he removed his tie completely and attempted to control the insistent press of his erection against his inner thigh, as strong now as it had been then.

Why had he presumed that her age and innocence made her different from every other woman he had ever known? For they had only proved to be even deadlier wiles than the practised artifice of the coquettes he was used to, prompting him to spend time with her because she had made him think she was lonely. Making him believe her small cries of protest when he bought her that damn dress were genuine, and not the reverse psychology of a mistress-in-the-making.

His mind jumped to the moment two weeks later, when one of his maids had nervously approached him, telling him Miss Matteson had left a red dress behind. For one rare moment he had *actually* hoped he was wrong. Because leaving the dress was not the only thing that had surprised him about her reaction afterwards. If she *was* just like other women, why had she not hung around and pleaded with him to change his mind? Or at the very least milked him for another gift or two? Such questions had left him on the verge of admitting to himself that the true object of disgust was himself, for taking her virginity and pushing her away rather than facing his own guilt.

Until he had buried his pride and rung England—and discovered she was already on a plane to God knew where with her next lover! The evidence had been unequivocal—worse, even, than discovering she had wanted him for what he could buy her. She had made a sexual conquest of him! He understood then what that feeling was that he hadn't been able to lay his finger upon. No, she wasn't like any other woman he had ever met. She was a hundred times worse. And now here she was again, six years down the line, returning for no other reason than to get her claws on his cash. And hadn't she proved last night just what she was willing to do to get it?

Dante shifted his legs and tried to focus on perusing the lunch menu. Despite his belief in the importance of stopping to eat, he realised it was a long time since he had even sat down at this time of day. But then today was not panning out as his day usually did. His morning had been strangely unproductive, and he had found himself wondering if there was something he really ought to be going to Il Maia to do every time he'd looked at his schedule. One thing in particular had kept popping into his mind, and, hell, he probably should have done *that* last night. He could not have had a more enthusiastic invitation. That hot, responsive mouth, the small moan of pleasure as he had taken her in his arms that had seemed to break from her subconsciously. So the little witch still acted as if it was the first time that a man had ever touched her that way.

That was why she still got to him. Because she had fooled him, made him believe her little performance until he lost control completely. But never again. This time he was going to make her sorry for everything she had thrown back at him the day she had surrendered her virtue and tossed away the opportunity he had given her. She would live to regret making a conquest of *him*. He was going to have her on his terms—when she knew full well that doing so wouldn't gain her a penny, when she could admit she wanted him for no other reason than that if he didn't have her desire would drive her mad. And then he would get her out of his system once and for all.

* * *

Faye felt as if it was herself on the plate as she was handed stuffed tomatoes and instructed to take them to him. Apparently Signor Valenti was in no mood for mushroom risotto. The restaurant was as busy as, if not busier than, the night before, with executive men and women discussing business at every table. But despite the multitude of suits her eyes were drawn instantly to the brooding figure he cut against the window. It was like walking a gauntlet; his mesmerising eyes were fixed upon her, his potent masculinity coiled in that easy pose, belying his danger. He had planned this, of course. The irony of the moment. Yes, he still made her feel that everyone else but the two of them were invisible, but he had not one iota of respect for her now. Now it was as if he was the emperor and she some offering, his to sample or disregard. But she felt oddly removed from the Faye of all those years ago, as if for Matteson's she had grown another skin of responsibility and purpose that kept her from breaking down at this perverse distortion of her memories. Except her skin was not so thick that she was impervious to the physical effect he had upon her. It took all her effort to place one foot in front of the other, willing herself not to look down to check that her legs were obeying her scrambled brain as she approached him. She wondered whether she had remembered to breathe.

'I am getting a little *déjà vu*, Faye. Do you feel this also?' The lightness in his tone had returned, as easily as if he was remarking upon the weather.

'Well, it was only last night that we were here, Dante. I expect that's it.' She had no intention of letting on that the first time they had met still stuck in her mind. 'As for me, like I mentioned earlier, waiting tables is a forte I have already mastered. So it is not so much *déjà vu* as a common experience.'

He looked perturbed. 'You consider working at Perfezione

a common experience for the second time in your life, Faye? I pity the man who seeks to give you the uncommon.'

Was that what it had all been about? The Italian billionaire bestowing a special experience on plain little Faye, whose life was a *tabula rasa*, just longing to be scrawled upon? Heaven forbid she should have felt anything as human as desire.

'I do not rely on men to fill the meaningless void that you consider my life to be, Dante.'

'Really? You just rely on them for money—is that it?'

Faye was still holding his plate a few inches away from the table. Although she stood taller than him he still somehow dominated her. His six-foot-five frame was at ease, like some predatory animal ready to pounce on the elfin prey in front of him. What was the point in arguing with him? Telling him that the idea of using men for money disgusted her, that this was the first time in her life she had ever asked any man for help? After her actions yesterday he was hardly going to believe her. Better he think that than know the truth. Her weakness would give him too much satisfaction.

'*Buon appetito*, Signor Valenti. Enjoy your meal.' Faye placed the plate in front of him, flashed him a counterfeit smile, and made to walk away.

'Have you eaten?' he asked, as though the thought that she was human had only just crossed his mind.

'You mean I am allowed a lunch break? I had no idea your terms were so civil.' She turned back to face him.

'Sit down, Faye. Eat with me.'

'Why?' It was ludicrous to feel so threatened, but she did. The question took him aback.

'Because we are both hungry, *cara*.'

He flashed her a look that was loaded with sensual promise, sending her senses into overdrive.

'Thank you, but I will have something with Lucia,' she replied calmly. 'Get to know life below stairs. Isn't that why I'm here?'

'Then just have a coffee,' he suggested casually, as she watched him take a sip from his own cup, which looked minuscule in his large hand. Her eyes were drawn to the sprinkle of dark hair at his wrist against the white cuff of his shirt, and then to his lips. She remembered how they had tasted her own, how it would feel to taste them again. She shook herself.

'I have just had an espresso that Bernardo made for me, thank you.' She saw him flex his other hand momentarily. 'I'd better be getting back. I am sure it does not project the right image, having a waitress loiter around for too long as it is.'

'I think you can leave it up to me to decide what image is Perfezione,' he murmured, so that she only just caught his words as his eyes undressed her with a single look.

'I would hate your tomatoes to get cold. Please excuse me.'

The rest of the afternoon passed in a blur of speed. Faye had gone back to the kitchen feeling as if she had just completed an endurance test, and then taken a quick break before promptly returning to work. By the time she was back on the restaurant floor Dante had already gone, the absence of his proud, dark head oddly conspicuous. Lunch at the restaurant had lasted several hours, and had been closely followed by a new flux of people arriving for coffee. At five o'clock, when the evening staff arrived, Faye felt dead on her feet, and after the restless night and the events of the day she was delighted to be able to slip away.

Tempting thought it was to go straight up to her room, her

unexpected need to remain in Rome longer than she had anticipated left her needing some supplies, so she went straight to the *supermercato* to pick up some basics. On the way there she passed the hotel's outdoor pool, and looked longingly at its shimmering depths. Faye had not swum competitively since her teens, but it was something she loved to do regularly. It gave her time to think, and not to think. The latter of which she suspected would be essential over the coming month. So when she spotted a fuchsia-pink bikini in one of the less expensive boutiques on the way back to the hotel—although never usually prone to impetuous spending—Faye treated herself. Believing she was only going to be here for a day or two at most, she had barely brought more than a few changes of clothes, let alone a swimsuit. Think of it as necessary for your sanity, she told herself. But much as she longed to change into her bikini at once, to go and release the frustrations of the day, she supposed she ought to check that Dante didn't mind her using the pool first.

As she whipped up a quick chicken salad and sat back to admire the view of St Peter's Dome from the balcony, she could not help wondering where he was this evening. Having dinner? Probably, and she doubted he was alone. Lucia had discreetly mentioned that he rarely dined at Perfezione, and that twice in as many days was unprecedented, so perhaps he took his other women elsewhere, somewhere more private. Not that she cared. The peace was a relief. She was just wondering because she didn't know what he had planned for her next, and she wasn't used to living like that.

The trill of a phone ringing broke her thoughts and almost made her leave her seat. Was it coming from the room next door? She hadn't even noticed a phone in here, though she supposed there must be one somewhere. She followed the sound, which led her to a table in the bedroom that she had not really noticed, and picked up an ultra-modern device.

'Hello?' There were only two options. No one but Dante knew she was here. So either it was a wrong number, or—

'Where were you?'

Or him. His voice was a low growl and it licked through her body. She leaned against the wall. Where was she? What kind of a question was that?

'Working, Dante. You employed me, remember?'

'After that.'

'What do you mean, after that? I didn't finish until gone five.'

'And now it's seven-thirty. I've been trying to call you.'

'I went shopping. Was I supposed to inform you if I left the building?'

'Don't be ridiculous.'

Look who's talking, she thought. 'I have to eat, Dante, or had you forgotten again?'

'And you mean to tell me you weren't tempted by any of the boutiques along the way?'

Faye was furious that technically speaking he was right, but not in the way that he thought. She was glad he was not there to see her cheeks burning.

'Anyway, that's precisely why I was trying to call. I'm having dinner sent up to you. I'm on my way to Lazio and won't be back until tomorrow night.'

'Thanks, but I've already eaten.'

The silence suggested it was a rare thing for his plans to be thwarted, even if it was something so minor. Either that or it had never crossed his mind before that women were capable of fending for themselves. She suspected his next question would be whether she'd eaten her five portions of fruit and veg, but if it was he didn't voice it aloud.

'Tomorrow Lucia will talk you through the importance of seasonal produce to our menu, amongst other things. In the evening we have an event to attend.'

'What sort of event?' she asked, hearing nothing but *we*.

'The Harvest Ball.'

Did all ridiculously gorgeous billionaires attend a school where they were taught to drop bombshells like that into everyday conversation? The Harvest Ball: an internationally renowned event that was like the Oscars of the hotel and restaurant industry. The one Chris was always talking about, and which he could only bear to miss if he was soaking up the sunshine on the opposite side of the world.

'How is that beneficial to my training, Dante? Surely it is nothing more than a glorified party.'

'If that is what you think, that is precisely why you need to attend. In reality it's a marketplace—work under the veneer of pleasure. It will be exceptionally beneficial to you.'

Work under the veneer of pleasure? A good description, Faye thought.

'Will I not hinder your negotiations?'

'Every man there knows a beautiful woman at his side is an exceptionally useful tool—almost a prerequisite, so to speak.'

The flutter of pleasure that had risen treacherously in her chest sank like a hot air balloon that was out of gas. How stupid of her to think even for a second that perhaps he *wanted* her there. Why did she keep forgetting it?

'I will be back in time to collect you at eight.'

'I have nothing to wear.'

'And didn't I know you'd be only too quick to point that out, *bella*? You will have, I promise. Remember what we learnt last night? You must be patient.'

And with that he rang off.

CHAPTER FIVE

THERE was something different about the room. Faye sensed it the moment she opened the door and slipped off her shoes, grateful for the feel of soft carpet beneath her feet after her second busy day in the Perfezione kitchen. But she was not able put her finger on exactly *what* was different until she entered the bedroom. And then she saw it: a large, cream rectangular box that under normal circumstances would have been completely conspicuous. But what was normal about anything that had happened in the last forty-eight hours? So, Faye thought, the answer to who he expects me to be at the ball tonight lies within that box. She looked around the room, wondering if he had been there. No, she reminded herself. Aside from being away on business, Dante would not concern himself with delivering an outfit for her himself, when she was nothing but a mere *accessory* for the evening.

She remembered his mocking comment about her impatience, and made a point of getting herself a glass of water and tidying a little before allowing the box any of her attention. Whatever was in it wasn't important. He would no doubt have asked whichever stylist was currently at his beck and call to send something over, the way he probably did for any woman he took out, so as to be sure she didn't show him up. He probably wished he had done so the night they had eaten in Perfezione. Perhaps that was the reason why he had had them seated at the most secluded table there was.

Sitting down on the bed, she inspected the box, running her finger across the luxurious embossed surface with a sense of foreboding. Funny how he could even make a gift feel like shackles. But she was unable to quell her curiosity. Removing the lid revealed swathes of soft tissue paper, and slowly, slowly, she peeled the layers back. What she saw underneath made her recoil in horror as the years fell away. Faye jumped up from the bed as if the dark red fabric she had revealed was poisoned. It might as well have been. Her dress. The dress he had bought her that afternoon in Piazza di Spagna—the dress she had been wearing when he had looked at her as if she was the most beautiful woman on earth. The dress she had left behind the day her heart had been torn in two.

The thought of putting it on again made her shudder, and she crossed her arms close to her chest, suddenly cold. So he had kept it. Why? It made no sense. Dante was hardly a man who needed reminding of his conquests with such tokens. And she was sure it was not because he might have qualms about the money he had spent on it. No, it was as if he had kept it knowing that she would return one day, determined to make her wear it as a badge of her depravity. She could not let him see that he had got to her, she thought, as she leaned over the box and tentatively picked up the garment by the shoulders. She held it up and let out a sigh. The galling part of it was that it was still the most beautiful dress she had ever seen. The colour was deep maroon, but not a single shade at any one time; it changed in the light, rich and lucent, like her favourite garnet earrings. She recalled the way it had made her feel when Dante had insisted she try it on; utterly feminine, alive, sexy. As if she was dressing up as someone else, because *she* would never have any occasion to wear it. Until now.

Two hours later, having showered and piled her hair in loose curls upon her head, Faye stood in front of the mirror wearing the gown. She had forgotten how much the shade suited her, having rarely brought herself to wear it since. And if she had worried about not fitting into the same size she had worn at eighteen, she needn't have. The places she had grown shapelier only served to improve her silhouette. The neckline scooped elegantly over her high, full breasts, and the tailored cut enhanced her small neat waist and curved softly over her hips, until it fell in luxurious flutes over her strappy shoes. Despite her initial reservations, she could not help smiling at the result as she put on her favourite earrings and finished applying her mascara. It had been a long time since she had dedicated so much time to her appearance, and she would never normally make herself up so—well, provocatively. But if Dante thought for one second he could unsettle her with this allusion to the past, then she was going to make sure it was he who was going to find himself out of his depth.

'Miss Matteson? Mr Valenti instructed me to inform you that the car is waiting directly outside.'

The man she had come to recognise as the reception manager greeted her as she stepped from the lift and led the way to the door, holding it open for her. She knew it was futile—knew there was no point imagining that this evening was anything other than business—but she could not deny the thrill of anticipation that shot up her spine as the driver held open the door of a long, black car. The sky was a beautiful mix of darkness tinged with apricot and orange hues. It was a balmy evening, and she could smell all the warmth of the September day that hung in the air. The inside of the car, with its black leather interior, was awash with shadows, and as she carefully sat down she did not immediately notice the still, unwavering presence on the other side of the seat until he spoke.

'Have you not got a wrap of some sort?' His question came out of the darkness, his tone accusing.

'I don't believe one was provided. But it is a mild evening, is it not?'

'Yes, it is. In fact I would go so far as to say it is *too* warm in here. But that is not what I meant.'

She saw Dante try to stretch his long legs out in front of him, as if he was uncomfortable. The streetlight was throwing his formidable features into relief, and his eyes were examining her with the intimacy of a touch.

'I had not recalled that dress being so…'

'So what?'

'So revealing.'

Faye could not help breaking into a smile that began at the corner of her mouth and lifted slowly to her eyes. She turned her head to the window as the car drew away.

He was evidently displeased. 'Does something amuse you?'

Faye looked back at him. His mouth was a thin, hard line, his features the picture of disdain. 'Not at all. I was just thinking that if this dress *were* revealing, which is hardly the case, it would provide exactly the distraction that you seem so eager to create.'

Faye thought she heard Dante mutter something in Italian under his breath, but she could not be entirely sure as they zipped along the main roads to the converted theatre where the Harvest Ball was held. He did not speak to her for the rest of the journey; the result was an atmosphere even closer than the night air. But Faye tried to ignore it as she switched her attention to the landmarks of the city as they flew past the window, conjuring up half-forgotten memories.

When they finally reached a standstill outside the impressive stonework building—so impressive that if she had not been consumed by nerves she would have felt the urge to whip out a sketchbook—she felt her optimism devoured by apprehension as she caught sight of the huge crowd of the elite. Could she be any more out of her depth? She was expected to rub shoulders with people who attended events like this every night of the week all over the world, when on any other night of the week she would be one of the dozen waitresses circling with canapés. But if Dante thought she would stick out like a sore thumb he didn't show it as he got out of the car and came to open the door beside her, offering her his hand. It was idiotic to feel weak at the gesture. His perfect manners were as inherent within him as his Italian roots. And yet Faye could not help feeling a surge of pleasure as she placed her hand in his. He curled his fingers gently and protectively around her own, and for a small moment the gap between them, as wide as the Mediterranean, felt a little bit smaller.

Standing beside him, bathed in the orange glow of the sunset, she felt the full force of Dante in his pristine black dinner suit and bright white dress shirt hit her. He was magnificent; his broad, hard shoulders and narrow, lean hips had her lips parting subconsciously, and the expensive fabric of his trousers with their thin vertical line seemed only to highlight rather than cover his taut, muscular thighs. He looked regal, and yet possessed a natural ruggedness that suggested he wouldn't have a second thought about crumpling every inch of his suit given the opportunity.

In the car he had been folded into the seat like a caged panther, unwillingly restrained in the shadows, unused to being out of the driving seat in every sense of the word. Now he stood tall, each one of his six feet five inches exuding a magnetism that had the women in the crowd looking longingly out of the corners of their eyes and the men subconsciously straightening their posture in a worthless attempt to assert themselves beside him. Faye reluctantly remembered how wonderful it had once felt to be by his side because he wanted her there, however temporarily. It had not been the envious glances of other women she had enjoyed that day in Rome. It had been knowing that this man, whom she admired so much, had chosen to spend time with her. She drew in a deep breath; now was not the time to get sentimental.

Dante led her swiftly through the grand doors, the heat of his hand creating havoc on her skin, domineering and yet oddly reassuring as they entered the throng of the party. The ornate walls and ceiling were bedecked in gold, and the heady scent of expensive perfume mingled with the sound of air-kisses set her head spinning. She watched him beside her, the consummate professional, as he weaved through the crowd, making brief and polite greetings, stopping at those people who clearly meant something to Valenti Enterprises in whatever capacity—to make introductions.

And Faye held her own in spite of her nerves, making polite conversation as she sipped the rosé wine he had handed her, grateful to discover that small talk was still small talk, even in the company of some of the world's wealthiest people.

Only Dante didn't seem pleased. Even when she swallowed her natural instinct to stand her ground, and took a step back to allow one woman after another to approach him and whisper something indiscernible in his ear before sashaying away with all the subtlety of a bird of a paradise. But finally she saw the hard lines of his face break into a soft smile as a woman with long, dark hair and a dress of midnight-blue approached them.

'Elena,' he said. 'I am so glad you could make it.' The woman's broad smile mimicked Dante's, her eyes alighting on Faye. Dante turned to her. 'Faye, meet my sister Elena. Elena, this is Faye.'

Elena nodded warmly, as if in recognition. 'A pleasure to meet you Faye,' she said in perfect English, offering her hand.

'Likewise,' Faye replied as she did the same, feeling immediately comfortable with the beautiful Italian woman who had the same sophistication as her brother, but coupled with a homely air that Dante lacked.

'I am not quite sure what possessed Dante to bring you along to an evening of what boils down to overdressed business negotiations, but I am glad to have a comrade.'

Faye laughed. 'Me too,' she admitted.

Dante seemed to spot someone in the distance as the two women exchanged pleasantries. 'Excuse me for just a moment,' he said, nodding towards a large group of black suits on the other side of the room. 'I won't be long.' His hand brushed Faye's arm before he moved off, sending a rush of heat through her body.

'My husband, Luca, is somewhere over there too,' Elena said, looking in the direction Dante was headed, out across the grand room. 'I told him I'd be happy to stay at home and look after Max to save on the babysitter, but he insisted on bringing me along.'

And Faye bet it wasn't because he considered her a useful tool, she thought, observing the look of adoration in Elena's eyes. She was surprised how natural it felt, standing here talking with her as they watched the men, as if she and Dante really were a couple. She felt as if she needed to explain that their situations were far from comparable, but Elena did not give her the chance.

'Dante tells me you're doing some work for him?' she asked with interest. 'I understand marketing is your speciality, so you probably feel much more at ease here than I do.'

Whatever Dante had told his sister about her, it obviously hadn't been strictly accurate. 'I'm just here for a month,' she said, as Elena smiled at her, 'and I'm afraid my marketing experience is on a much smaller scale than this.'

'I'm sure it is still fifty times greater than mine!' Elena laughed. 'I haven't a clue, and to be honest Luca's equally out of his depth, but since we bought the farm in Tuscany he's expected to be here.'

Faye could just imagine Elena in a farmhouse, surrounded by crops and animals and children. She did not know why the image filled her with a dull pang of wistfulness, why the incongruous image of Dante in a similar house seemed to pop into her head.

'Faye?'

She heard her name being called from somewhere on the other side of the room, interrupting her thoughts. The voice was familiar, but it took until she swung round to face him for her to place it.

'Chris!'

Dressed as fashionably as ever, and sporting his trademark Californian tan, Chris leaned back. He looked her up and down, then nodded his head approvingly before kissing her dramatically on both cheeks.

Faye embraced him affectionately before introducing him to Elena, who smiled genuinely, seeming to sense his instant likeability which was as striking as his boyish good looks.

'I thought you were still in the States?' Faye exclaimed, her mind still playing catch-up. The last time she had spoken to Chris had been six months ago, when she had called him about Matteson's. She knew he had no money of his own to invest after blowing his inheritance on his ventures abroad, but his father had been a friend of her parents for generations, and for all his impetuous spending she had always valued his refreshing eccentricity and loyal friendship.

Chris rolled his eyes and let out an enormous sigh. 'No such luck! I spend years researching American cuisine to take it back to the British public and what do I discover? It's conventional old Europe which sells! So here I am—for the next few months, at least—soaking up the restaurant scene in Roma.'

Faye laughed at the way he made it sound as if the results of his research were a surprise, and as if being here was such a chore. He had never looked more at home than amongst the world's fashionistas, and had waxed lyrical about Rome's Harvest Ball being *the* event of the year for as long as she could remember.

'But never mind about me. Tell me what on earth *you* are doing here, and who is responsible for this *fabulous* transformation! You look positively *glowing*.'

Faye stifled a blush, aware of Elena looking on, and ignored Chris's implicit but harmless criticism of her usually subdued wardrobe.

'It's not what you think,' Faye said, shooting him the kind of look only an old friend would understand. 'I'm just here in connection with a possible investment in Matteson's.'

'And who could refuse you in an outfit like that?' He winked.

'Quite.'

Dante's voice sliced through the air behind her. She had no idea how long he had been standing there, but when she spun round his face was as dark as deadly nightshade.

'Dante!' Faye did not know why she should feel as if all the breath had been whipped from her lungs, but she didn't like it. She fought to fix a smile on her face. 'You remember I told you I went travelling to the States?' she said, as casually as her voice would allow. 'This is Chris. He's now doing some research here. Chris, this is Dante. Dante—Chris.'

Faye watched the two men shake hands as the orchestra began to strike up, thinking that the two of them meeting was like a double bass meeting a tambourine and clashing on sight.

But Chris seemed oblivious, looking at Dante in awe, as if he had just announced that Elvis had entered the building. 'Dante *Valenti*? I'm such a fan of your restaurants—*so* inspiring.'

'Even for conventional old Europe?' Dante said sardonically, proving he had probably heard the entirety of their exchange. 'Elena, I believe your husband is looking for you,' he shot out abruptly, before he jerked his head round to face Faye. 'Care to dance?'

His tone left Faye in no doubt that it was an order, not a request. Chris seemed to willingly recognise his cue to leave, and directed a shrewd look at Faye accompanied by a friendly nod which said, 'Don't worry. I understand.' *If only he did understand,* thought Faye, as the haunting melody of a tango began to strike up. *If only I did.*

Dante did not wait for her assent, but led her to the floor. A few other glamorous couples were moving the same way. She did not kid herself that this was anything but an exercise to ensure he was in control of exactly where she was and who she was talking to, but nevertheless to think of Dante dancing for any purpose seemed at odds with everything she knew of him. It seemed too expressive, too meditative, to be something he would find time for in his fast-paced, work-obsessed life.

'Do you always dance at these occasions?' she asked as he snaked one hand around her waist and placed her own hand upon his shoulder. Awareness shot through her the minute his body came into contact with her own.

'Never,' he drawled, his mouth disturbingly close to her ear as he took the lead, making her feel so light it was if he had changed the force of gravity.

She had danced with men before, of course, at university. So why did it suddenly feel as if she was experiencing the pleasure for the first time? As if all of a sudden she understood why people described it as sensuous, erotic? Because you're dancing with *him*, a voice said in the back of her mind. Because this isn't a minute of ungainly swaying with some guy who seems to hear *yes, please* instead of *no, thanks*. This is dancing with Dante Valenti, who is as proficient at this as at everything else he touches. Like Midas, she thought as they moved in time to the sultry rhythm, feeling as if she was turning to molten gold beneath his fingers.

'You *never* dance at these occasions?' she whispered breathlessly. 'Then how did you get so good?'

She felt him tense slightly. 'Some things come to us instinctively, wouldn't you say?'

So he was reluctant even to discuss something as innocuous as where he had learned. Because small talk with *him* wasn't part of this deal?

'You are talking about sex, I suppose?' Faye shot out, fired by a need to bring down the barrier he had put up in front of his emotions, and only realising once the words were out of her mouth just how risky it was to articulate the image she didn't seem to be able to budge from her mind.

'Ahh, Faye, you speak of it so matter-of-factly for a woman.'

'*For a woman?*' she asked incredulously. 'Is it not a fact of life when two people want one another?' She was all too aware that she had steered the topic of conversation into dangerous territory, and that she was speaking on a subject upon which she could hardly be any less of an authority, but his misogynistic comment irked her.

'And you have always been so clear about your wants, *bella*.' His voice was loaded with suggestion, his thumb moving provocatively in small circles on her back as he moved them deftly around the floor. So he still thought every woman who wasn't a nun was as good as a harlot, she thought, cursing him.

'And what of *your* wants, Dante? Oh, but of course—you are a man. So you are not only permitted to have such indiscretions, you celebrate them. Heaven forbid a woman should do the same!' Faye did not know quite whose corner she was arguing, but his double standards made her blood boil.

'So you wish to celebrate your sexual triumphs, do you, Faye?'

Why had he supposed that bringing her here would be any

different from when he had let her loose in his kitchen? He thought. To her this was just a bigger playground!

His voice was acidic as he continued to manoeuvre her across the floor, his languid movements replaced with a precision and sharpness that suddenly made her aware of her own inadequacy.

'Does it thrill you to think there are two men in this room tonight you have given yourself to? Or perhaps there are more?'

His arms opened in disgust as he spoke the words, releasing her from his punishing embrace, and although he moved towards her once again she took a step backwards, too insulted to continue.

'Perhaps there are, Dante. Who knows?'

And with that Faye turned on her heel, losing herself in the crowd as the orchestra beat out the song's climactic ending.

'I apologise for my brother.'

Elena found Faye queuing at the bar—for the want of something to do to prevent herself from looking round to see where Dante had gone as much as for needing refreshment after the heady experience of that dance.

'Sorry?' Faye said, suddenly terrified that even half of what they had been discussing had somehow carried across the dance floor.

'The way he felt the need to "rescue" you from your friend. Dante is a very possessive man where the women he cares for are concerned.'

Faye nodded, thinking that it didn't matter whether he *cared* or not. Possessiveness seemed the order of the day.

'You can imagine what he was like when I had my first boyfriend.' Elena laughed. 'Luca was the only one he deemed even remotely suitable after months of scrutiny. Which was convenient since I'd already agreed to marry him long before I told Dante.'

They had just made it to the front of the queue when Luca found them both, and Elena made the necessary introductions.

'It's a pleasure to meet you, Faye. Any woman who can get Dante on the dance floor has clearly made an impression on him.'

Faye was not surprised to find that Luca shared the same look of adoration for his wife as she did for him. But when Luca curved his arm protectively around Elena, Faye was unprepared for the pang of jealousy which hit her. Funny how no matter how used she got to being alone something so small had the power to remind her of what she didn't have.

It soon transpired that Luca had finished the networking he admitted was a necessity of the evening and had come over in the hope that Elena was ready to go home. Elena protested that they could not leave Faye alone, or go without finding Dante, but Faye convinced them that he had no doubt just stepped outside, and that she would find him immediately and pass on their farewells rather than them having to negotiate the now-busy dance floor to reach the French doors which led out onto the terrace. Reluctantly they agreed.

In truth Faye had no such intention; she had told herself she would find Chris, catch up on old times and leave Dante to his own black mood. But as she stood alone, watching the couples twirl hypnotically across the floor, something more powerful determined her path.

The back of the theatre was surrounded by a large oval veranda with wrought-iron railings that reminded her a little of the foyer at Il Maia, and somehow she knew immediately that her instincts about where he had gone were right. As she stepped out of the enormous doors she felt surprised there were not more people taking a break from the evening's festivities, but as she moved farther away from the warmth of the party cool night air nipped at her skin.

He must have heard her footsteps approaching, but he did not turn around. She could see from his pose that he did not want company, and felt instinctively that to go to him now would be to dice with danger. Yet as he stood there, like some devastating gothic hero, a picture of strength and solitude in the dark shadow of the evening, she was drawn to him. Slowly she walked towards him, the cool wind playing with the honey coloured tendrils of her hair that had worked their way loose.

'Go back inside. You'll catch a chill.'

'The change of scene is refreshing.'

'And yet you seemed to be in your element.' He remained focussed on the dark hills in the distance.

Her eyes flicked over the profile of his face, the high bridge of his nose, the hard jut of his jaw, fortified with a tension that refused to dissipate. She realised she had never seen him look *so* Italian.

Faye did not answer him. She had done exactly what had been asked of her—mingled with his associates, his sister and brother-in-law—yet somehow she had still ended up riling him.

'Elena and Luca asked me to pass on their goodbyes.'

He nodded, as if it went without saying.

'I liked them very much.'

The comment seemed to surprise him, and he snapped out of his dazed look, as if the idea of her having any affable feeling was impossible. How little they really knew of each other, she thought, a shiver rushing over her.

In an instant his jacket was off and he was behind her, draping the heavy fabric around her shoulders. His heady, musky scent surrounded her. It felt so intimate, and yet everything tonight seemed just the opposite. Faye tried to ignore the distracting sensation of having him behind her, turning her eyes back towards the people indoors.

'You never told me where you learned to dance like that, Dante.'

There was silence for a moment, and then he said, 'My mother.' His tone was curt, and he turned back to face the darkness of the night sky.

Faye immediately sensed that it had not been a pleasurable experience and did not push him. But slowly he continued.

'Let's just say she was something of an expert on the *advantages* of frequenting every ball in every hotel in Europe. She made me practise with her.'

Faye knew little of Dante's childhood, and what she did know was only from what the papers said about this self-made billionaire. According to them, his mother had died before he was in his teens, and he never spoke of his father. After her own secure and loving childhood, she could only imagine the horrors of the experience his brief but telling words hinted at. What would that do to a young man? Faye wondered. No wonder he had been so protective of his sister.

'I'm sorry,' she whispered.

'Sorry for me, or for my mother?' he asked, turning on her.

Faye frowned softly. The revelation which seemed to have dulled her own anger had plainly had the opposite effect on him. 'For you, Dante.'

'Why? When tonight you have proved just what an expert you are in exactly the same field? How does it feel, Faye, to

pout your lips and know every man is wanting you? To walk
across the floor ticking off each conquest in your mind, planning the next?'

She almost wanted to laugh at just how wrong he was, how
unfounded was his sexual jealousy. Yet the realisation that *that*
was what all this was about made her anger return. *He* didn't
want her, but still he was so chauvinistic that he didn't want
anyone else to have her either. It cut her to the quick.

'You think working with men is synonymous with sleeping
with them?'

His face was the picture of distaste. 'No, *bella*. I *know* it
is where you're concerned. How else do you explain why you
begged me to make love to you and only a fortnight later you
were *working* halfway around the world with a man who still
can't keep his eyes off you?'

Faye stared at him, knowing she should retaliate but too
dumbstruck by the fact that he was saying things he couldn't
possibly know.

'How did you know that?' Her voice was low, urgent. 'I
never told you when I went travelling.'

There was silence for a moment.

'Let's just say I made a call to be sure I was right about
you. One of your colleagues kindly informed me exactly
where you were. Did he offer a higher price for sharing his
bed, Faye?'

She shook her head in disbelief, her eyes focussed on the
hard stone beneath her feet. The furious shade of molten gold
that burned in his eyes was too dangerous for her to look at.
He had called and she had never known. The revelation was
like an ice-cold shower down her spine. And yet did it really
make any difference? He had made up his mind about her long

before that. What good would it do to tell him now that she had gone to escape her feelings for him? What good, when the only way to escape the pain was to keep those exact feelings locked away?

'A shake of that pretty little head of yours means nothing, princess. But let me guess. You can't look me in the eye? Now, why might that be? Because you're a damned liar, perhaps?'

'Why can't I look into your eyes?' she questioned desperately, her voice racked with emotion, her breathing rapid. 'You want to know why?'

She lifted her head to meet his gaze and her body began to tremble.

'Because I'm afraid that if I start I won't be able to stop.'

CHAPTER SIX

SHE was right. As her wide, fearful eyes met the onyx-dark depths of his Faye was lost. But if she had thought that he would accept her words as proof of her innocence, the unforgiving set of his features told her that he did not. He might be the expert on change, but he was no more capable of opening his mind to the truth than she was capable of looking away. It struck her that if anyone had come out onto the terrace they would have thought the two of them were lovers, locked in an embrace of requited love and contentment, and she wasn't sure whether that made her want to laugh or cry.

There was no question of what was coming. No wondering if he would or he wouldn't. But it would hold not one inch of affection. The suggestion of tenderness—his jacket around her shoulders, the soft curve of his lower lip, the languorous spreading of heat throughout her limbs—were all part of fate's joke at her expense. Yet she could not deny that she longed for it to come, as if it was the air she needed to breathe to stop herself from fading away.

She did not know how long they stood there, with the cool breeze of the evening beginning to whip around them, each defying the other, unmoving. But the moment their defences shattered was sudden and mutual. Hungry and reckless, his lips crashed down upon her own and she pressed her body wantonly against him: the culmination of anger and of hurt. Was it possible all those years ago he had regretted his words? Had tried to reach her and found her gone? No—and even pondering that question would be a terrible mistake. Worse even than entwining her tongue with his now, as it slipped in and out of her mouth, promising intimacies of a much deeper kind.

His kiss was condemning and furious, as if it sought to erase everything but the wanting between them. Until suddenly he dragged his mouth away. For one hideous moment she feared he was going to take his revenge by rejecting her again. But if that had been his intention his self-control had failed.

'Home. Now,' he bit out, his voice throaty, his need obvious.

He did not wait for her agreement; he read it on her face. Words were unnecessary as he led her artfully to the front of the building, via a side passage that avoided the crowded dance floor, and took them straight to a waiting taxi as if he had willed it into existence.

They sat deliberately on opposite sides of the back seat, both knowing they didn't dare go near each other—yet. *Not long now*, his eyes seemed to say to her, looking, if it was possible, even more predatory than they had when he had arrived. She ought not to continue to feel like some startled gazelle, yet somehow she felt even more apprehensive than she had at eighteen, when she'd had all the daring of youth and been blissfully unaware of the fallout that would follow. Ever since desire and recklessness had been words that had virtually slipped out of her vocabulary. Until now. Now they were written in bright red ink across her mind, obliterating the fears scribbled beneath. And never had she so longed to give in to those words as she eyed him hungrily, imagining his tanned hands against her pale skin, on her breasts, *lower*.

Home indeed, she thought, with desire unfurling deep within her. But as she turned to look at the moon, low in the sky, she realised that they were not headed in the direction of Il Maia, and that there was only one other home he could have meant. *His* home.

Her heart thrilled at the thought of the intimacy of arriving at his domain, though she knew really that he was simply bringing her there because it was the most discreet and sensible option. Yet she was not sure sensible applied in any way to her state of mind as he paid the taxi driver and whisked her up the steps to the luxurious apartment block that was tucked away in a quiet and exclusive street just outside the city centre. His was the top two floors, naturally, but the detail of the layout eluded her as he led her through the expansive rooms, his hand upon the base of her spine playing havoc with her grasp on anything except the feel of his body in contact with her own.

He did not turn on the lights, and Faye felt the butterflies in the pit of her stomach multiply. Moonlight was streaming through the enormous glass windows, projecting the shadows of their bodies onto the wall. How many women had he brought here? And how much more skilled in giving him pleasure must they have been than her? Was it even possible that he wanted her—she who had displeased him so much before? For nothing had really changed. Because, whatever he presumed, after her moment of naive boldness had proved to be such as disaster, sexually she had retreated back into her shell. A shell that no one had been able to prise open since. So why did it seem to *fall* open for him?

'You hesitate, Miss Matteson?' His eyebrows were raised in mock rebuke as she wavered at the foot of the stairs, running the tip of her tongue over her lower lip nervously in a movement that drew his black gaze. 'Surely not?'

It was the moment to stop—the moment to walk away and end this ridiculous charade right now. But she couldn't have even if she had wanted to. As she stood in the dress he had bought her, the jacket he had cocooned around her, with the delicious taste of him on her swollen lips, she did not even feel the decision was her own. It was as if her fate, however cruel, had been decided long ago.

She shook her head.

'Then touch me,' he commanded.

And she understood what he asked—knew that this was about *him* possessing *her*, on his terms. But for once in her life she didn't give a damn about whether that was right or wrong. Because she could ponder that as long as she lived, but not acting now would be to deny herself the only thing that made her feel truly alive.

She reached up her arms in willing surrender, entwining them around his neck, running her fingers greedily through his thick dark hair, glorying in the feel of it as she pulled his head down for a long and lingering kiss that was hot and wet. His lips found her neck, below her ear, and his warm breath sent her senses haywire as he trailed feather-light kisses lower. Emotions rushed over her like a wave; she was unprepared for such tenderness amidst their mutual urgency. Deftly, he threw his jacket from her shoulders and ran his hands over her as they sank down together on the stairs. Slowly, he discarded one flimsy strap of her dress, peeling back the dark red fabric from her naked flesh to reveal a thrusting nipple

which peaked expectantly under his gaze. Faye let out a sigh
of need that was matched by his exhalation of breath as he
took it in his mouth and ran his tongue slickly over it, causing
her to grip on to the stairs for dear life.

'Not fair,' she cried out breathlessly, her hands tugging at
his tie, which she removed with ease, pulling it impatiently
from under his collar and letting it fall to the floor. She
relished the feel of unbuttoning his shirt. But before she could
finish he caught her hands in his own and held them behind
her head. A bubble of excitement broke from her throat.

'Not fair?' he questioned silkily, raising his eyebrow in
challenge. 'I completely agree.'

Faye expected him to remove his shirt for her, but he did
nothing so self-centred. He revealed her other breast in light-
ning-quick time and treated it to the same sensual exploration,
his left hand stroking the other. She had never been so turned
on in her entire life as she lay there, her evening dress exposing her to the waist, her body crying out for more and more
of the man who held her captive with the sheer force of the
yearning he stirred within her. But more than that, it felt as if
dreams she had never believed herself capable of dreaming
again were being handed back to her, piece by piece. De-
lighting in the realisation, she arched her back to allow him
to take more of her soft peak into his mouth, one of her hands
still tangled in his hair, encouraging him.

'Dante!' She guided one of his hands lower down her body.

'Patience, Miss Matteson,' he said, lifting his head, a mis-
chievous glint in his eye as he replaced his hand on her shoulder.

The allusion to exactly why she was there and at his bid-
ding ought to have set an alarm bell ringing through her, but

the idea of him bestowing more pleasure upon her silenced it before it even rang.

'Stand for me,' he ordered, allowing her the space to do as he requested, lying back on the stairs lazily to watch her, propping himself up on his elbow.

She did exactly as he asked, only realising as she did so the consequences of her actions. The dress that had gathered at her waist slipped effortlessly to the floor, leaving her standing there in nothing but her flimsy lace panties and her despicably high-heeled shoes.

Dante muttered something indiscernible in Italian and was at her side in a flash, sweeping his warm hands under her bottom and lifting her up into his arms.

'If I don't get you to the bedroom right now,' he ground out, 'you are going to have some nasty carpet burns on this delectable body of yours.'

In no time at all they had reached the top of the stairs, and he carried her towards the master bedroom, where an enormous bed made up with pure white cotton sheets was just visible through the darkness. He laid her down with the utmost care, his gaze lingering upon her body. She liked the way he looked at her, as if he almost—no, as if his need for her was the one thing he couldn't control. It might not be the way a man gazed at the woman he loved, the way she gazed back at him, but she knew that at this moment he wanted her, and it was enough. Because he was Dante, whose hard, rugged body had filled her dreams for so long. She kneeled up on the bed provocatively.

'Now, let me finish what I started, Mr Valenti.' She cocked her head as he stood looking down at her, and moved to unbutton the rest of his shirt.

'My thoughts exactly, *bella*.' Though her hands stalled for a moment, as she realised she had insinuated more than she had meant to, she had no intention of stopping to reflect. She stripped his chest bare and sat back on her knees, looking him up and down with sultry eyes.

'You have no idea how much it turns me on when you look at me that way,' he murmured as her tongue subconsciously went to the roof of her mouth.

Her lips parted as she eyed every inch of bronzed flesh and rigid muscle, sprinkled with whorls of dark hair. She moved towards the edge of the bed as he lay down beside her, the throbbing heat of his desire pressing against her stomach through his dark trousers.

'Please,' she cried raggedly, pressing herself into him so her nipples grazed his chest as she moved her hands clumsily to discard the remainder of his clothes. He took over the task for her, deftly removing both his trousers and his shorts, his proud, hard length springing free. Her breath caught in her throat at the sight. She was sure she was not supposed to find it so beautiful, but the undeniable evidence of his masculinity, so smooth and hard, did things to her insides. More things than she dared admit even to herself. She reached out to touch it, but he moved away.

'Ladies first.' He smiled wickedly, the moonlight throwing his striking face into relief.

Ever the gentleman, she thought, as his finger trailed over her flat stomach and hesitated for a moment on her inner thigh before casting aside the small scrap of lace. She let out a small cry as he dipped one finger inside her and then began to circle rhythmically, sending tremors through her body that slowly sent her higher and higher. She saw the satisfaction in his eyes as he watched her clasping herself to him, but she wanted him to share the pleasure—to feel as helplessly bound to her as she felt to him. She reached out, wrapping her hand around his hard shaft, and heard him groan.

'Do you have any idea what you do to me, *cara*?' His accent was stronger than ever as she stroked his length, matching the rhythm of his hand at her feminine core. And though his tone held a note of all too familiar condemnation, it made her realise that for all his demands she held the ace. He wanted her, whether he wanted to or not.

'I have an idea what I am *going* to do to you,' she said seductively, placing one leg on either side of his taut body, her boldness returning as if it couldn't help itself when faced with *him*.

His eyes suddenly shot open as he realised what she was about to do, and for one terrible moment she thought he was going to stop. 'Wait,' he said, one arm reaching across to the bedside table, and in one swift movement he protected himself.

Ever the professional, she thought. But then all thought was swept away as he ran his hands over her hips and encouraged her downwards, entering her in one hard thrust. Faye's body opened for him invitingly, welcoming him home as if created for him alone, and she wondered deliriously at how, despite her being on top of him, he had still managed to take control.

Determined to regain some power, she moved above him, slowly dipping up and down on his length, and the pleasure in his eyes was palpable as she built a slow and steady rhythm that he matched with his own hips. Gradually she picked up the pace, sending them both to a place without language, with only feeling and sensation. The realisation that she was making love to Dante all over again, was connected to him in the most inseparable way there was, filled her with as much heat as the physical pleasure of having him inside her. She did not know how she held off her climax as the intensity grew stronger and stronger, but as she watched his face, knotted with passion, she was determined to make him lose his grip on reality first. As she heard a low groan beginning to break forth in his throat, and felt his movements reach even deeper, rubbing against the sensitive folds of the innermost part of her, she could not hold on any longer. Her own cry of ecstasy was matched by his as he made his release, sending them both over the edge, shattering into a thousand pieces like a firework lighting up the night sky.

And for the most perfect moment he held her there, in a gesture which seemed the most tender she had ever known, his arms wrapped around her as their breathing slowly grew more steady, like two people attached to parachutes who were floating back to earth. Flooded with so much emotion, Faye felt inexplicable tears prick at her eyes—the spontaneous kind that no one ever warned you to expect.

But with her eyes still closed she realised that for the second time in her life she had landed in the all too familiar territory of limbo-land, where she didn't know what she was supposed to do or say *afterwards*. Only this time there was no future to misconstrue. For though *she* felt as if she couldn't have acted any more impulsively, she realised with a jolt that all she had really done was live up to everything he had expected of her from the minute she had walked into his office three days ago. The realisation made her open her eyes suddenly, and the tangle of their bodies, with her limbs on top, only served to remind her exactly how *thoroughly* she had proved him right.

'There is no need to feign surprise on my account,' he murmured, his eyes barely open. 'We both knew it was on the menu.'

Faye didn't answer, but freed herself from his embrace. Once he had made her feel embarrassingly brazen. Now she just felt embarrassingly predictable. *But alive*, a voice inside her head whispered in her defence; *you made your bed, now lie in it*. So she did, perfectly still; not a single part of her touching a single part of him. And as he made his way to the bathroom she realised that remaining detached was the only possible hope she had of seeing this contract through.

Dante was not gone for long, but when he returned she was dead to the world. The role reversal made him uneasy. Most women usually swanned off to the bathroom to reapply their make-up afterwards, leaving *him* to fall asleep. Not Faye Matteson.

But then she was all about contradiction, wasn't she? He stood a metre or so away from her. Her sweet fresh scent was like an aphrodisiac lingering upon his skin, and one honey-coloured strand of hair stroked her cheek lightly as she breathed slowly in and out. She looked almost *vulnerable*. And knowing what a lie that was didn't banish the unfathomable discord in his chest.

It was not disappointment. Heavens, no—that had to be some of the best sex he had ever had: the responsiveness of her hungry lips upon his own, the way she had whispered his name like a siren song and wrapped those extraordinary legs around him. This was what he had planned, after all.

Yet it hadn't happened *how* he had planned. Yes, that was why it hadn't put an end to that old feeling he couldn't put

If offer card is missing write to: Harlequin Reader Service, 3010 Walden Ave., P.O. Box 1867, Buffalo NY 14240-1867

NO POSTAGE
NECESSARY
IF MAILED
IN THE
UNITED STATES

BUSINESS REPLY MAIL
FIRST-CLASS MAIL   PERMIT NO. 717   BUFFALO, NY

POSTAGE WILL BE PAID BY ADDRESSEE

HARLEQUIN READER SERVICE
3010 WALDEN AVE
PO BOX 1867
BUFFALO NY 14240-9952

his finger on in the way he had expected it to. For he hadn't counted on dredging up his past. Nor had he expected her to frustrate him to such a degree that he had been almost unable to prevent himself taking her there and then, at the most sophisticated ball in Rome. How many men had she ensnared with that enticing body of hers? he wondered. Using that facade of virtue to ensnare her victims like a spider weaving a web of deceit. Why had she even bothered to argue against what he knew to be true? And *why* had he felt that wretched swelling of guilt all over again when she had shaken that angelic little head of hers? *Dio!* He knew it was all an act to turn him on, and she had damn well succeeded!

He drank in one last look at her before turning back to the door, furious that his moment of pleasure was tinged with such frustration, furious that what he wanted most was to rouse her from her sleep and take her again and again. But that would mean relinquishing control, and Dante never relinquished control to anyone or anything. Least of all to a woman who was only after his money and had just slept with him to get it.

Sweet autumn sunshine poured through the wide glass windows, gently rousing Faye from her languid slumber. She stretched out her arms as wide as they would go, as if she was some synchronised swimmer, keeping her eyes closed. She froze as she reached the pinnacle of her tautness, realising just how far her limbs had stretched without meeting the edge of the bed. This was not *her* bed. Which meant only one thing. She kept her eyes shut, willing either the faint tenderness between her thighs to dissipate, or the hand that was frantically searching the empty space next to her to rest on him. But neither. She opened her eyes to find herself alone, and realised that she had no way of knowing whether Dante had even come back to bed last night at all. She had fallen straight to sleep as he had headed for the bathroom, and she hadn't stirred until now. For all she knew he could have retired to one of the other bedrooms.

She stared at the empty space beside her, trying to discern whether it was body-shaped. Could this whole scene be any more clichéd? she thought. The room spelled bachelor pad. The whitewashed walls, the dark angular furniture, not a family photo in sight. What had made her think for one moment that waking up next to the enigmatic Dante Valenti was any more likely now than it had been six years ago? She closed her eyes again and drew in a deep breath, sitting up and leaning back on the obscenely comfortable pillow. Yes, this was all too familiar—and there was no way she was going to stick around and endure a conversation like *that* one again.

But just as she was about to alight upon a plan for slipping away from him unnoticed, the bedroom door slowly opened. As she scrambled for the duvet to avoid exposing herself, she wanted to yell that he should have knocked—until she remembered that was this was his apartment, and had he not snuck away he would be lying there naked with her.

But he wasn't; he was already dressed for work, looking despicably handsome in a pale grey suit and a white shirt with dark pinstripes. He was missing only his tie, and even the slight shadow at his jaw that she had felt against her skin last night was shaved cleanly away. The only anomaly was the steaming mug of freshly ground coffee he carried in one hand.

'Thank you,' she said tentatively, accepting it from him.

'There are fresh croissants downstairs.' The timbre of his voice was as unfathomable as the look on his face.

Was this one of the perks of a one-night stand with Dante Valenti, then? Mind-blowing sex with an emotion-free continental breakfast included?

She composed herself. 'I can be ready for work in half an hour.'

'You surprise me.' He cocked his eyebrow sardonically.

'Like you said, *that* isn't going to get me my money any quicker.' She gave a brittle laugh. At least the cutting remarks were something she was accustomed to dealing with.

His face turned to thunder as he paced over to the window. So he was furious even though she had acknowledged that last night didn't change their deal? There was no pleasing the man.

'Then you should be able to catch the eleven forty-five flight to Tuscany,' he said, still focussed on the city view.

'Tuscany?' Faye could not hide the surprise in her voice.

'I have arranged for you to meet some of my suppliers there. I had planned for you to go next week, but I see now that today is just as convenient. It is a unique opportunity.'

'You are going there on business?'

'No.' The sunlight seemed to have faded, the room no longer so warm. 'I have meetings here.'

He would be here. She would be gone. Suddenly breakfast felt like the booby prize.

'They speak English?' Faye questioned, wondering if the practicalities had eluded him in his sudden desire to banish her from his sight, and determined to alight upon some get-out clause.

'Some. But my sister will accompany you anyway.'

'Elena?'

'Yes. She lives near to my villa. You may use the facilities whilst you are there.'

He made it sound as if the concession could not be more repellent to him. She supposed now he had taken what he wanted he had no other way of disposing of her between now and the end of their contract. Faye stared at him, not sure why she wanted to ask him how long it would be before she saw him again, and cursing her treacherous heart for feeling only that she would miss him, rather than hating him for toying with her all over again.

'Elena will meet you at the airport and take over things from there.' He tossed her some keys. 'I will leave the flight details on the table downstairs. Lock the door as you leave.'

And would you like me to carve an extra notch on your bedpost for you? she wanted to fire back at him, but he was already out of the door.

CHAPTER SEVEN

It WAS her second day here in Tuscany, yet Faye could still scarcely believe that the man who owned the stark, clinical apartment she had been left to dispatch herself from just thirty-six hours before also owned *this* room. She adored it all: the warm cream walls, the natural fabric of the terracotta suite, the understated olivewood furniture. It was spacious, of course, but not excessively so. In fact the one word she would use to describe the place was homely. And as she looked out at the groves of citrus fruits and cypress trees visible from the wide living-room window, the image of Dante at a family home in the country that had popped into her head at the Harvest Ball no longer seemed so illogical. But it was delusional, she reminded herself, because he'd made it perfectly clear that, regardless of how he kept his house, he ran his life like a business: supply and demand. And the minute she had willingly given in to his demand and supplied him with her body he had made it plain she was surplus to requirements.

Thankfully this was the first opportunity she had really had to dwell on that since she had arrived. When she had got here, late yesterday afternoon, Elena had collected her from the airport, bursting with enthusiasm to show her the countryside, and their scenic journey back to the village where Dante's villa was located had lasted until it grew dark. Beset with the sheer exhaustion of travel and the events of the night before, Faye had fallen into a deep sleep until Elena had called early this morning for her to begin their tour of the producers. From that moment on her day had been too full of this bittersweet utopia for her to completely succumb to the visions of Dante still dancing through her mind.

But whilst the part of her that faced the world felt truly in awe of the things she had seen—ripe figs being plucked from the trees, fresh cheeses being pressed—underneath she had never felt so utterly raw. And now she was alone she was forced to confront the rejection that she had once promised herself she would protect her heart from feeling ever again. Yet even though she reminded herself that she had gone into this knowing what the outcome would be, no amount of reasoning made it any easier. Nor did being apart from him, though on the plane journey here she had told herself it would be preferable to staying in Rome. Quite why, she wasn't sure, when even going to America before hadn't made a blind bit of difference. But she hadn't expected to find it *harder*—to feel his presence everywhere.

Elena spoke to Faye as if she was practically Dante's wife-to-be, rather than some redundant mistress. And each place they went it took only one mention of his name and the same look of reverent adoration crossed people's faces, as if he was not just part of the community, but some kind of local deity. The very notion was completely alien to Faye. This was the man who was as changeable as the wind, who got through women like cups of coffee, but the connections he had here were plainly loyal and longstanding. Perhaps he paid these people extortionate prices for their goods? But that still did not explain their steadfast pride when talking of their involvement with Signor Valenti.

'It must be a great contrast for Dante when he comes here from the city,' Faye had suggested to Elena casually, desperate to grill her on the two personas her brother seemed to have without seeming discourteous. But Elena had only shrugged, nodding as if it was no big deal.

This evening Elena was otherwise engaged, and Faye had been looking forward to having some time to herself, to explore the villa and its grounds. The darkness when she had first arrived, along with her early start this morning, had offered her little opportunity. Only now was she beginning to wish that she didn't have such a long night ahead of her to sit and think, surrounded by evidence which suggested that somewhere in that hard but delectable chest of his he had a heart. How much easier it would be to sit in his dispassionate apartment in Rome, believing the space beyond his ribcage was empty.

She twisted in the armchair, thinking how little compassion he had shown *her*. Or had he? He had made it clear from the moment he had taken her to dinner that he fully intended to have her and then let her go. Inwardly, she castigated herself. She had stupidly believed that their conversation at the ball had changed things, that just for a second he had let her in. But here she was, banished from his sight all over again. She drew in a deep breath. How long did he intend to leave her out here? The entire month? Was it devised to be the ultimate torture—being left to imagine what it would have been like to be one of the women he usually accompanied here, forced instead into exile with only her memories for company? She cast her mind over the events of the last few days, trying to convince herself that all was not lost, that this was actually what she had wished for: to sit out the month quietly, until she could get the money Matteson's so desperately needed. But as she touched her fingers to her lips she could only think of needing him, of the taste of perspiration on his skin, of how it would feel to take him in her mouth...

Good God, what had he done to her? She who prided herself on qualities like restraint and self-control. Qualities? Or were they barriers to hide behind? she wondered ruefully. All the time too scared of getting her fingers burned? But if they were the only scars that being around Dante Valenti left her with then she could cope. The trouble was he set her whole damn body aflame, and she needed to cool off.

Faye had spotted the inviting waters of the Olympic-sized pool from her bedroom that morning. Yes, she thought, convincing herself that aside from needing to douse urges she had never known she possessed, it would be a practical way to fill her time, release some of the tensions of the past week and to be sure she was physically tired enough to be guaranteed the release of sleep. She was thankful now that she had had the foresight to buy that bikini, however guilty he had made her feel about it at the time.

It was 5:00 p.m. and the air was beginning to cool as Faye made her way out onto the terrace and tentatively approached the edge of the water, testing it with her toes. To her delight the temperature was glorious, the heat of the sun having warmed it perfectly during the day. She plunged in gracefully, entering the water like some sleek mermaid, barely causing a splash.

The silence was utterly calming and tranquil as she began to swim from end to end, losing herself in the rhythm of the strokes. There was none of the crowds or noisy echoes she was used to contending with at her local pool, only herself, the water, and the beautiful backdrop of acres of green. She swam as she had done as a child, without inhibition, as if only the motion of her body mattered, not caring how many lengths she pounded out, knowing only that she would stop when she was ready and it wouldn't be any time soon.

That was until she felt the air change halfway through one length in the direction of the villa. Though she told herself there could be no distraction, she felt compelled to open her eyes.

'Making the most of the facilities, I see.'

The deep, sardonic voice broke across the water at the exact moment Faye laid her eyes upon the imposing masculine body at the edge of the opposite end of the pool, shocking her out of her meditative state with a start. The previously still water flew in all directions as she struggled to regain her composure and began treading water. Though droplets laced her eyes she did not for a second need to speculate as to who it was. Apparently her body didn't either. Her stomach felt as if she had just taken her first mouthful of food after days without eating. She hadn't realised until now just *how* hungry for the sight of him she had been.

'What are you doing here?' The words broke from her huskily.

'I live here, or had you forgotten?'

Forgotten? She thought. *I can barely think about anything else.*

'I thought you had business in Rome.'

'It's the weekend. Surely that hadn't escaped your notice?'

'I was working today,' she answered automatically, as if he wouldn't have known.

'I am well aware of that. For you it is essential. I, on the other hand, am not the one who needs to learn.'

Maybe you need to learn *you* can't treat people like this, she wanted to retort, as she clasped her hands around her body, suddenly aware of just how intently he was looking at her. It was just beginning to grow dark, and the faint lights around the pool gave the air a smoky quality. It drew her attention to the irresistible tanned skin of his muscular arms beneath his black T-shirt, and highlighted the taut contours of his patrician face. She noticed his hand move as she pushed her mane of water-logged hair from her face and wiped her eyes. Hell, he was taking the T-shirt *off*.

'What are you doing?'

'What does it look like? I'm joining you for a swim.'

A million thoughts flashed through Faye's mind—*He knew I was here. Maybe once was no more enough for him than it was for me? But this is his home, and me being here is inconsequential, isn't it? What good would more than once do anyway? It would only make things harder.* But her reasoning came to a standstill as she watched him fling the T-shirt to one side. Harder indeed.

Faye wanted to escape, and swim closer to him all at the same time. As she dragged her gaze over his magnificent chest and down to his lean hips she longed to run her hand over his taut stomach, to feel her body pressed close to his all over again. He removed his dark jeans in one swift movement and she felt something she erroneously branded as relief when she saw he was wearing swimming shorts, however brief, beneath them.

He dived proficiently into the pool, and Faye's senses were heightened as the ripples reached her. Her body thrilled just at the knowledge that he had entered the same expanse of water. She felt her nipples harden involuntarily beneath the surface, despite the warm temperature. His head came up a few metres away from her.

'When I heard you splashing about in here I thought perhaps I might have caught you skinny-dipping,' he said, his voice low, his face close to the water. 'But it seems that sadly I was right about your shopping extravaganza in Rome.'

'And what makes you think I didn't bring a swimsuit with me?' She angled her head defiantly whilst avoiding his gaze.

'Because I know you, Faye,' he said, sending a chill through her with a look that seeped deep into her soul. 'And, much as I like the idea, I don't think stripping down to your bikini in my office was plan B in getting me to show an interest in your offer.'

'High praise indeed. I thought that was precisely what you thought of me.' Was he actually beginning to believe otherwise? She felt herself weaken.

'Well, if you care to prove me wrong,' he whispered, moving slowly towards her, 'please feel free.'

'I wouldn't dream of it,' Faye answered, mock demurely. 'Even when I thought I was completely alone I was being a good girl, doing lengths in my perfectly modest two-piece.'

'Is that what you call it?' he asked, raising his eyebrows skeptically. His face was now so close to hers that she could see the rivulets from his damp hair running slowly over his broad shoulders, as if wavering in order to allow her lips the chance to kiss them away.

'Precisely,' she said standing up so her bikini-clad breasts met the water level. 'And since I was unprepared for an intrusion, I think perhaps I will retire to my room.' She began to move towards the steps.

'I don't think so.'

He offered her no chance to escape, stretching out a single arm and encircling her waist, holding her fast. She gasped, the sudden close contact startling. As he twisted her round to face him one of the triangles of her bikini top slipped sideways. It was only when Dante's gaze dropped to her exposed breast that she noticed, flailing her arms to re-cover her proud, exposed nipple.

'And this is what you call modest, is it?' His voice was grim, and Faye flushed as she straightened the offending fabric—though she could not help noticing the way his tongue met his bottom lip unconsciously as she did so.

'I cannot be responsible for its effectiveness when I am being manhandled, but as a piece of swimwear I consider it is perfectly reserved.'

'I'd sign Il Maia over to you this instant if you could find me one man on this earth who would agree with you on that. But then you do have the ability to make a sheet look like lingerie. No reason why a bikini should be any different.'

Dante's arm still held her, and as he spoke her eyes fell to his mouth. There was no denying the hunger she read there, and no denying to herself how much she wanted him—in every way it was possible for a woman to want a man. His hands toyed deftly with the strings that held the offending clothing in place, and she arched her back as the top fell readily into the water, freeing her to the cool night air. Even the moment it took for his warm hands to come forth and cup her eager breasts seemed too long, but as his thumbs began to circle the tender buds in the water she knew she would wait for ever if he asked her.

'Dante,' she whispered. The hypnotic motion coupled with the lapping water was sending shock waves to her inner core, willing greater intimacy. She was grateful for the buoyancy of the water, for without it she was sure she could not have remained standing. The thrill of his hands on her body, his presence after missing him more than she dared admit, overwhelmed her. And the eroticism of having him strip off her bikini right here, in the water, drove her to distraction.

She felt the heat of his arousal and reached her hand into the water, holding him through the thin fabric of his shorts.

'You see now how I know it is improper?' he ground out, indicating the thin scrap of pink that was now the only barrier between her and her nakedness.

'I can't miss it,' she replied huskily, a smile spreading across her face as she gloried in the feel of him touching her, in the knowledge that, whatever else was true, he had come because he wanted her as much as she wanted him.

He whisked away the tiny bikini bottoms in one swift motion and brought her legs around his waist. His hand made a small but thrilling journey from her inner thigh to her honeyed warmth, open for him, and he began to concentrate his slow, steady movements. Faye had never felt such intimate sensation, never known such wild abandon. His mouth went to her nipple, revelling, kissing and teasing as he continued his expert exploration below the water. Somewhere in the recesses of a mind swamped with pleasure she realised that he must want to satisfy her, that he could take her right here in the water but was choosing to bring her to her own point of ecstasy rather than satiate his own obvious need. Her shock and elation at such consideration reminded her of her own inexperience, but was instantly replaced with a sudden and foolish wonder at what pleasure it would be to come home here to this, every day for the rest of her life. But her body was too receptive to his touch to allow any thought, futile or otherwise, to remain in her mind for long. And as his slow movements brought her to her peak, every nerve-ending and emotion rose to the surface. She clamped her mouth down upon his shoulder in sheer ecstasy, the aftershocks convulsing through her body.

'That was…' she whispered as the water stilled around them, almost too overwhelmed with emotion and disbelief to find the word '…remarkable.'

'You sound surprised,' he ground out, as if his prowess usually went without saying.

'I've never done that before,' she said quietly. 'Just me, I mean.' She was sure as hell it would inflate his ego, but right now she was past caring. She was too infused with satisfaction.

'You mean your other lovers have been selfish?' Dante said, his words stunted. 'Then they are fools.'

He did not give her a chance to correct him, thought she hardly saw what difference it would make if she tried. He had already made up his mind about her six years ago.

Dante launched himself out of the pool, his pressing erection still evident as he passed her a towel. 'I'm hungry,' he said, and Faye wanted to smile at the irony, but his expression was severe. 'Get changed. I will make us some dinner.'

When Faye emerged from the shower twenty minutes later, she was mystified by the myriad of delicious scents wafting from the kitchen. Old-fashioned, homely smells—that word again. They had to eat, of course, and his knowledge of excellent food went without saying, but the thought of him actually cooking surprised her. And what was more he had decided to get creative in the kitchen *now*, after they had just been

intimate. Could it be any more different from the last two occasions when they had made love? When what had followed
was him ensuring she was as far away from him as possible?
Faye tried to quell the ludicrous excitement that zipped
through her. For, as experience had taught her, dinner was
likely to be just another step up from the morning-after breakfast, and he was about to dispose of her all over again.

'There's some clean clothes in the wardrobe, *cara*.' His
voice rang through from the kitchen as she was towel drying
her hair, contemplating the inscrutability of it all.

Faye wandered over to the large mirrored wardrobe, his
words not really sinking in. As she opened the doors she fully
expected to see nothing but the grey suit and the couple of
other casual numbers she had been surviving on. But the rail
was full of outfit after outfit of beautiful clothes. For one
naive moment she wondered if Elena had sent some over for
her to borrow, but as she picked out a white linen skirt and a
raspberry-coloured top she saw the tags: they were all brand-
new, and designer to boot.

Faye exhaled through her teeth. So that was what this was
about. When Dante had demanded that she become *his* for the
month he had meant it. His to control, to make helpless at his
touch whenever it suited him, to dress in whatever he wished.
That was why he was here now.

'Put them on.' His voice echoed through to her, as if he had
sensed her hesitation through the wall.

She shivered as she held up the outfit in her hands and
compared it to her tired clothes squashed together at one end
of the rail. Yes, it was easy to *reason* that the whole set-up
went against everything she believed in, but why did it have
to *feel* so damn good?

'Is this really necessary?' Faye strode into the room, trying to ignore the delightful swish of the new skirt against her legs as he swung round to face her, saucepan in hand. She was momentarily taken aback by the way steam rose from the hob, causing one strand of his dark hair to flop distractingly across his brow.

'*Bell-a*,' he said, pronouncing it so deliberately it sounded like a caress.

The look on her face pleased him. It had frustrated him that she hadn't made a single protest about being brought out here when all the while he had been in Rome, at war with his libido over how many days to keep her dangling. Finally her perplexed little pout felt like a victory.

'The fortune that little lot cost would no doubt have gone a long way towards the refurbishment needed at Matteson's,' she said, attempting reprimand but suspecting she was failing miserably as her heart softened at those two haunting syllables.

'Ahh, Faye,' he said softly. 'Still you underestimate the severity of your financial problems.'

'No, I'm just saying I could have managed on the things I had.'

'Surely you are not suggesting that clothes are not a requirement of this month, *cara mia*? Because if you are I might have to make you prove it.' He broke out into an irresistible smile and Faye knew she had lost. 'It wouldn't be fair to expect you to survive on the things you brought for only a short trip,' he said, turning back to the hob, 'and I promised I would provide everything you needed whilst you are here.'

Whilst I am here, thought Faye, realising how easy it was to forget that before long she would be back in England and, aside from the money and that ridiculous profit target to meet,

it would be as if she had never been here at all. To him, at least.
So why didn't she start being the woman whose point of view
she had argued at the ball? Just because she was female it
didn't mean she couldn't enjoy a purely physical relationship
with him until it was time to go their separate ways, did it?
She watched him deftly tossing vegetables in the pan. Yes, that
was the only way to deal with this. Live for now, she thought.
Dare to change your stupid obsession with the consequences,
take a leaf out of his book and treat this as though it's perfectly normal.

'Do you cook often?' she said, a little too unsteadily to pass
for *normal*, as she fetched cutlery from the sideboard and
began to lay the table, already bedecked with a beautiful
burnt-orange cloth and candles burning at either end.

'When I'm here, always.'

'The rural way of life inspires you?' Faye queried, trying
hard to connect the quintessential city-slicker with the image
before her.

'My grandparents' way of life.'

Faye stopped arranging the place settings for a moment and
looked up at him, unable to disguise her curiosity. 'They lived
in Tuscany?'

'Yes, in this house. I grew up here.'

'I didn't realise.' Faye was taken aback. It seemed to explain
so much, and yet at the same time to raise even more questions. From what she had gathered he had spent the early part
of his life trailing after his mother from one city to the next.

'Elena and I moved here after my mother died. I was
eleven—'

It was telling that he defined from that moment onwards
as his *growing up*.

'That can't have been easy.'

'Easier than you would think.' His voice was flat. 'Every-one who knew my mother thought she was destined to die young. She was—how is it you say?—like a moth to a flame, drawn away from the country to the bright city lights in search of rich men.' His lip curled in distaste. 'Children were no more desirable to her than growing old would have been.'

Faye frowned, unable to comprehend how any woman could lack basic maternal instincts. 'And your father?'

'Who knows?' He shrugged in a gesture that was exagger-atedly Italian, though his muscles were a little too taut for it to pass as customary indifference. 'Perhaps not even him.'

Faye sensed her cue to change the subject. 'So this is where you began?' she asked, spinning around on her feet, taking in the kitchen, imagining him here as a young man.

'Before I lived here, sitting around a table to eat was some-thing I had only seen other people do through restaurant windows. As for preparing food itself, I knew even less.'

'Your grandparents taught you to cook?'

He nodded, as if the cooking part went without saying. 'They taught me how much it mattered. I made sure I never forgot.' He shrugged again. He made it sound easy, but she knew better than most how hard this business was, how tire-lessly he must have worked to create an empire based on nothing more than that belief. She realised she had never admired him more.

'You must miss your grandparents,' she said, wishing she could do her father even half as proud.

'What they taught me about the meaning of sitting down and eating good food remains.'

Faye was not sure she had ever felt so close or so distant

from him all at the same time. In one sentence he had summarised exactly how *she* felt about Matteson's, and explained the roots of his own motivation which she had never fully understood. But suddenly she also saw how his need for change and his grounding in the things he was passionate about could co-exist. The Dante of Rome and the Dante of the Tuscan hills. Yet what was *this* whole set-up all about, when she seemed so clearly to fit into the *destined for change* category?

'And what about eating with me? What does that mean?' Faye's voice was quiet, as if she hadn't really meant to speak her thoughts aloud.

Dante looked up, any emotion that he had unwittingly allowed to creep onto his face replaced with a wry expression. Her words sounded suspiciously familiar to him, like those used by women who mistakenly supposed that when he released some detail about his life it put their relationship on a deeper level than sex. But this was Faye Matteson. The chances were *that* was exactly where she wished to steer this conversation.

'It means we are two adults, with the same taste in life's mutual pleasures.'

'You once led me to believe we had tasted all that was worth savouring.' Faye lowered her head.

'You want to hear me say that I still burn for you, *bella*. Is that it?' His voice was loaded. 'You are tired of hearing of my past, and instead you wish to know that around you I find my appetite is insatiable?'

Faye shook her head, trying to ignore the dart of pleasure that shot through her. She motioned to her clothes, the dinner. 'No. I just wonder where the word "mutual" fits in to all of this.'

'You are trying to pretend you are not crazy with longing

too, *bella*?' He mocked. 'After earlier tonight? You needn't bother. Even with your vast experience you must admit the sexual chemistry that exists between our bodies is rare.'

'That's not what I meant. I mean—me having no say in any of this.'

'But isn't that exactly what turns you on, Faye?' He looked at her mercilessly as she blushed. 'As well as precisely what you signed up for? For, despite all your protestations of female supremacy, doesn't knowing I might take you right now drive you wild?'

Faye tried to look away, but he reached his hand across the table and tilted her chin so that she was looking straight into his ebony-dark gaze.

'And when I do you will beg for me to do it again,' he murmured. 'Are you foolish enough to argue that I am wrong?'

Faye could make no answer. Her body had reached its own conclusion.

'Then I suggest you put down that knife and fork.'

CHAPTER EIGHT

IT FELT like a sexual awakening. Yes, they had made love before he joined her in Tuscany, but that night something changed. It was as if they had both surrendered to what Dante had described as the 'rare chemistry' between their bodies. To Faye, his analysis sounded painfully like the narrative in a science textbook, but, paradoxically, it somehow rationalised things in her mind. As if the only way to deal with the desire that existed between them was to live for the moment and savour it in exactly the way he described.

And savour it they did. For not only had Dante's words broken through her defences, but he seemed determined to prove just how *mutual* their needs were. And for the next few days, as if she was on some delicious sensual voyage, she learned for the first time in her twenty-four years what it was to exist in a world where there was only you and your lover. The kind of experience she supposed her friends had been having with boyfriends for years. Where you didn't ask questions like, *When is this going to end?* or *Shouldn't we be at work?* The kind of relationship that his rejection six years ago had ensured she'd never got close to. They were shut away from the rest of the world, learning each other's bodies, discovering a whole new scale of sensations. She could barely recall what else they did with their time but make love, wherever and whenever their desire struck them, with breakfast becoming brunch, only stepping outside to cool off in the pool or pop to the local shop for fresh bread and milk.

Watching the palpable enjoyment on his face, feeling him reach for her again and again, she found it astonishingly easy not to think about the consequences. It was only times like now, late in the night, as she listened to him sleeping, that questions began to grate on her. Like when would he be returning to Rome? Because today was Wednesday, and though he'd said he was only down for the weekend he was still here. She was desperate to ask, and yet it felt vital to her survival to pretend she didn't care.

'We will resume your tour tomorrow.'

His voice cut through the darkness. So he was not asleep. Faye felt her senses return to high alert, as if he had flicked a switch.

'Oh?' she mumbled, feigning drowsiness and wondering, not for the first time, if he possessed the ability to read her mind as well as the cravings of her body. Or had the undiscussed boundaries of the situation got to them both?

'You have much still to see, and I wish to visit some of my suppliers whilst I am here.'

'You no longer have pressing business in Rome?' Now it had arisen, she couldn't pass up the opportunity to discover if he had always planned to replace Elena as her guide, or whether it was the last few days that had persuaded him to alter his plans.

He moved towards her. 'I discover I have more pressing business here *at the moment.*'

It felt like a cleverly dropped reminder of her place in his 'temporary' file, and yet as he came closer her hormones went into overdrive, and all she could think was, *He's staying. I have changed his mind.*

'One of the perks of being head of Valenti Enterprises?' she asked lightly, telling herself to take his admission with a pinch of salt. 'A bank balance guaranteed to rise without any-one dictating where you must be and when?'

Dante stilled. For one long moment he looked at her through the dim night light as if she had said something in another language, and he was slowly translating and discov-ering the meaning was repugnant.

'Precisely.'

The moment he spoke the word it seemed to change the temperature in the room to an icy chill. He rolled away from her. The sudden sense of emptiness left her feeling utterly bewildered, and sleep was even further from her grasp.

Eventually, in the early hours, the pleasures of the day be-fore finally outweighed the disquiet of their exchange and Faye fell into a deep sleep. He was standing over her when her eyes flicked open.

'Finally she wakes,' he drawled.

'Sorry.' She reacted instantly, rubbing her eyes and sitting up, peering at her watch on the bedside table. Nine a.m. He was fully clothed, his arms crossed in front of him. It was a far cry from being woken up by those self-same arms snaking around her waist yesterday. Yes, *he* might be staying, but had *business Dante* returned?

'You should have woken me earlier.'

'Believe me, I was tempted. We leave in half an hour.'

Faye nodded and scrambled out of bed, momentarily for-getting her nakedness.

He threw a towelling robe in her direction. 'We won't be going anywhere if you continue with that,' he growled, determined to reassert some control. If she was going to make snide little comments that intimated that him telling her where to be and when was such a chore, she could damn well do some work. 'I'll meet you outside.'

Faye nodded obediently as he left the room. It was gratifying to know she turned him on—she couldn't pretend it wasn't, or that the feeling wasn't mutual. But far harder to deal with were all the other things she had discovered about him, just by living alongside him for this short time. Like the way he constantly surprised her.

When she slung her bag over her shoulder and headed out through the door twenty-five minutes later, determined that she would not provoke his mood any more than she'd had already unknowingly done, the last thing she expected was to find him with his legs slung either side of a gleaming black motorbike. So, she thought with bemusement, even his mode of transport outside of the city was simple, carefree, fun.

But if he noticed the look of pleasure on her face he ignored it. He was silent as she walked towards him, the sight of his body on the powerful machine, clad in dark jeans, a white T-shirt and a black leather jacket, causing somersaults in her belly.

'Put your arms around my waist,' he commanded, seeming to sense her ineptness. Though her not having been on a motorbike before wasn't exactly the reason why she was so frantically gnawing her lower lip.

She did as he told her and they set off immediately. Beautiful countryside zipped past, the wind whipped through her hair, and the press of her body against his powerful back as the machine roared beneath them almost pushed his black mood from her thoughts. For wasn't his unpredictability the very reason that being with him was so exhilarating?

And when they arrived at a vineyard she was reminded that she was far from alone in her admiration. For, though she was well accustomed to seeing women fawn over him and men pandering to his success, she had not expected the owners to greet him almost as if he was family, not in the least intimidated that the man responsible for their livelihoods had dropped in unannounced.

'Did your grandparents introduce you to suppliers in this area?' Faye asked, her curiosity too great to remain silent as they followed the old man down into the cellar. It occurred to her that she was as captivated by Dante at work as she was by Dante in bed. 'They treat you as if they have known you all their lives.'

He hadn't fully anticipated how bringing her here would only serve to reawaken her enthusiasm for every element of the business, and to remind him just why he had admired her so much when he had first met her in Matteson's all those years ago. It didn't sit well with him; much easier to believe her passion lay in one place alone.

'Some of them, yes. Others, like Grumio and his wife, here, I sought out because I tasted something so good that I wanted to serve it to others.'

Faye dropped back as Dante spoke rapidly to Grumio in Italian, discussing what looked to be a new red he had produced. And as his words sank in Faye realised with a start that it was exactly what he had done with her back then: spotted her talent and decided he wanted it for himself. But it made her feel as if *she* was wine being swilled in a glass, for what ought to have been the most positive, defining moment of her life had ended up as the complete opposite.

'Faye?' Dante beckoned her over to taste the deep purple liquid, and Faye was forced to snap out of her contemplation. 'What do you think, will this suit Perfezione as the new house red?'

Faye smelt the fruity aroma of the rich dark drink and took a mouthful, closing her eyes the way she always did, as her father had once shown her. She was grateful; it wiped out the enticing sight of Dante's fingers upon the stem of his glass and allowed her to form something like a coherent response.

'It's good.' Faye nodded as she opened her eyes. 'Not too heavy.'

Dante held his glass up to the light and nodded in agreement.

'But is it more expensive than your current choice?' she asked, looking down at the bottle on the table.

Dante turned his head sharply to face her. 'That is what Grumio and I were discussing. I will not make the switch unless it is like for like. Has your Italian improved?'

'Sadly not.' Faye shrugged. 'I recently decided to update Matteson's wine list. Unfortunately our merchant presumed we had made up our minds to make changes regardless of price, so I went elsewhere.'

Dante put down his glass, taken aback. He had supposed that she was keeping her pretty head out of it, hovering at a distance because the negotiations were out of her depth. He hadn't anticipated that the opposite was true, or being reminded that her talents in this business still existed.

'Very wise.'

He sounded surprised. She looked in the direction of the winemaker, taking the steps down to the lower cellar to replace an unopened bottle in the rack. That was it, wasn't it? If, like Grumio, she had been a *man* whose skills had impressed him back then, he wouldn't have doubted her abilities now. It suddenly dawned on her that a woman capable of business *and* sex appeal simply couldn't exist in his mind; the minute she had shared his bed, in his eyes she had become incapable of any other achievement. The reality of their differing ideologies slammed into her. She felt as if all this time she had been running blindly, assuming there was a finish line in sight, however distant, and now she had just looked down and discovered she had been on a treadmill all along. No matter what she did she would never change his cast-iron prejudice.

'Just because I am a woman it doesn't mean my father didn't teach me anything but how to wait tables.'

'I wasn't basing my assumptions on your gender,' he breathed. 'But on your track record.'

'Matteson's, or mine?' Faye shot back.

'Both.'

'You once wanted me to work for you, Dante.'

'And what was it *you* wanted? Let me think—'

'So because I made love with you it automatically transpires that I did not want to do anything else with my life from then on?' Faye interrupted.

'No, Faye. *That* transpired the minute you disappeared and—how would you like me to phrase it?—found an alternative *employer* within the space of two weeks.'

Grumio hovered awkwardly at the top of the stairs. Their expressions were no doubt as clear as if they had been speaking in his native tongue. It was tempting to yell back at Dante regardless, to blast his outdated views and to ask how *he* would have reacted if he had had to face the humiliation he had put her through, but it seemed pointless. He only ever dished it out. He didn't feel it.

Faye turned her back on him, knowing she was as likely to alter his viewpoint as she was to find a pot of gold at the end of a rainbow. What did it matter what he thought? She had faith in her own capabilities, and once she had the money she needed she would prove them. Instead she spoke to Grumio, as much from a determination to demonstrate her professionalism as to dispel the tension. *'Grazie, è squisito.'* Thank you, it's delicious.

Grumio bowed and spoke rapidly, obviously presuming her Italian was better than it really was. She only caught a couple of words. *'Bella...vostra foto.'*

Faye furrowed her brow, unable to fully comprehend and all the more frustrated for having no choice but to turn back to Dante.

His tone was clipped. 'He says it is his pleasure, for you are just as beautiful as your photo.'

Faye turned back to Grumio, still perplexed. *'Foto?'*

'In the newspaper.' Dante translated his response without waiting to be asked, shrugging his shoulders nonchalantly. 'It seems you are splashed all over the tabloids *cara.* Congratulations.'

'Me?' Suddenly it felt as if the bubble they had been existing in for the past few days had well and truly burst.

Dante ignored her look of horror. 'Did the myriad of flashes escape your notice when we arrived at the Harvest Ball, Faye? Surely not? The world's press are no doubt swarming over each other, trying to discover who you are.'

In the emotional rollercoaster that came with being around Dante she had forgotten that he was practically royalty when it came to the papers. It was stupid to have done so when she had seen so many photos of him with supermodels and A-list stars over the years. It was part of her daily routine to avoid the news stands on her way to Matteson's. She had just supposed that because this was nothing, because she was a nobody, they wouldn't be interested. And now it seemed that not only Dante but the world saw her as his mistress.

'I want to see them.' Her tone was demanding, edgy. It might be a day-to-day occurrence in *his* life, but it wasn't part of hers. God knew what the headlines said—what people back at Matteson's would think if they saw them.

'Just when you were doing such a good job of convincing us that business was your only priority.' Dante's mouth slanted sardonically, ignoring her request. 'We're finished here. Let's get something to eat at the villa before we head east to the olive groves this afternoon.'

He moved forward to bid a puzzled-looking Grumio a charming goodbye, leaving Faye no choice but to quickly utter *arrivederci* herself.

Why was it that the minute she consoled herself with faith in her own abilities something else transpired which seemed only to back up his derogatory opinion of her? And why had she played right into his hands?

As Dante led the way out, Faye lagged behind like a sulking child.

'I'm not hungry.'

'But let me guess—you would be suddenly ravenous if I suggested we go the café opposite the newsagents?'

'Is it a crime to want to know what lies they've printed?'

'Why? So you can sell *your* story in exchange for more cash and extend your fifteen minutes of fame?' he said, turning on her like a viper disturbed.

'Do you really suppose I would do something so degrading?'

'Do *you* suppose I am fool enough to believe that you are some moral high-grounder?'

'What's that supposed to mean?'

'It means that if you really were so *proper* you would have no reason to worry *what* they printed.'

FLAVOUR OF THE MONTH! DANTE VALENTI HAS MYSTERY MISTRESS EATING OUT OF HIS HAND AT ANNUAL HARVEST BALL.

Faye stared at the headline on his computer screen. The minute his phone had rung as they were finishing lunch she had seen her chance to slip away. He had given her permission to use his personal office to stay in touch with Matteson's earlier in the week; there was no reason why she shouldn't check the internet now. But with his accusations circling in her mind like a hungry shark she couldn't help feeling as if she was doing something forbidden.

Yet, more than that, as she saw herself through the eyes of the world she was forced to confront exactly what she had become. For whilst being around Dante made it hard to retain faith in herself and in Matteson's, or to believe that she was capable of the emotionless sex this bizarre situation demanded, seeing the words in black and white made it damn near impossible.

Dante's latest arm candy is thought to be an unknown Brit by the name of Faye Matteson, daughter of little-known late restaurateur Charles Matteson, whose once passable eatery has fallen on hard times. Whilst the appeal of Italy's richest and most eligible bachelor to Miss Matteson goes without saying, critics have been stunned by the über-hunk's departure from haute cuisine to what can only be described as pot snack.

The article was accompanied by two pictures. The first was of Dante, looking devastating but blasé as he ushered her into the theatre. Her expression was so startled and meek even she felt like giving herself a good kick. The second was a hazy photo of the two of them dancing, which was all the more erotic for its lack of clarity. The two of them together looked like some comic strip in which a poor little match girl looked up at an Italian billionaire with dollar signs in her eyes and decided to get raunchy. It made her stomach turn.

Not that she should have been surprised, of course. What had she expected? She *was* nothing more than his mistress, and though she might have told herself that she accepted that, she'd been wrong. Her one job had been to keep her feelings at bay, to live only in the present, and she had failed. Because she had found delight in much *more* than their lovemaking; she had adored hearing stories of his childhood here in the Tuscan hills, and meeting Elena and Luca, had relished sharing meals and ideas with him as much as she had savoured sharing his bed.

'Is seeing your name in print the thrill you were hoping for?'

Faye jumped up from her seat, the unexpectedness of his presence behind her causing a flush to her cheeks. She turned and shook her head, feeling as if she had been caught planting a ticking bomb. 'I have seen what I needed to see. Shall we go?'

'No.' For a moment his eyes licked over her in such blatant

sensual appraisal that she wondered if it had always been his intention to come home for more than lunch. But he continued. 'That was Elena on the phone. I've asked her over this afternoon to thank her for showing you around last week—and to see Max.'

Faye swallowed. He expected her to meet Max—another member of his family who in a few weeks would exist as nothing more than a memory of something she would never be a part of again.

'What about visiting the olive groves?'

'Like you said, one of the perks of my job is not having anyone dictate where I need to be and when,' he replied flippantly.

Faye knew in that instant she couldn't do it. Couldn't go through an afternoon of playing happy families. She was his *mistress*, and he would never see her as anything more, so why put herself through this added heartache?

'I thanked Elena myself, actually,' Faye said, taking a deep breath and rising from the office chair to face him full on. 'So if we are taking the afternoon off I think I will go shopping instead.'

'Do you indeed?' His voice was razor-sharp.

'Yes. Seeing these photos reminds me I have nowhere near enough clothes for the duration of my stay.'

His eyes narrowed. 'And what about the wardrobe full of clothes I provided?'

'Wardrobe *full*? Men never seem to realise the real extent of that concept.'

Faye did not turn to face him, but she could sense anger billowing from him like steam. 'You *will* be here when they arrive.'

'Why? Do you wish me to give the impression of being a permanent fixture in your life? Surely that demands a higher fee?'

'What are you playing at, you little witch?' Dante took one step towards her.

'Being your mistress, I thought.'

'And doesn't it come so naturally?' His eyes glittered as he flicked them first over her, then down to the headline on the screen.

'You should know, Dante.' Faye shrugged, picking up a pen and pretending to write a shopping list that came out as a garbled mess of misspelled designer boutiques she was grateful that he couldn't see.

'Why don't we put it to the test?' he said, his voice husky. 'Since you are so desperate to be treated like one.'

Faye froze. The pen was suspended between her finger and thumb like a pendulum.

'Take off your dress.'

Faye turned on one foot, like a netball player who had just been passed the ball but dared not move for fear of losing the game. 'What did you say?'

'You heard.'

Faye hesitated, her eyes darting to the clock, then back to him. But he was leaning rakishly against the wall, as if he had all the time in the world and would wait as long as it took.

'Concerned you'll lose precious shopping time, Faye?'

He was daring her to say yes. But though the word was on the tip of her tongue she was immediately consumed by something stronger than speech. The slow pulse at the base of her throat. The all-consuming need to have him look that way at all of her, to know he needed her as much as she needed him.

Though her mind fought against her body, Faye slowly raised her hands and began to undo the zip at the base of her neck. An exultant click issued from deep in his throat.

'And when you're done with that, lose your underwear.'

Dante pulled the chair away from her and sat down to watch. It was like being some exotic dancer. So exposed. And yet as she stripped down to her panties and bra she felt only exhilaration. Not just because she didn't know exactly what was coming next, but because now, when it felt as if they were worlds apart, the promised intimacy of their bodies was like finding a bridge.

Edging down one strap of the bra, she heard him release a low growl of anguish. If she had not been prey to her need to be close to him she would have teased him longer. She tugged the delicate French knickers over her hips and bottom, feeling his eyes follow the movement down over the length of legs that had grown bronzed in the days of Tuscan sunshine, and growing warm once more beneath his gaze.

'Come here,' he commanded.

She walked slowly towards him, reaching out to encourage the T-shirt from his jeans, running the flat of her hands over the naked skin beneath, watching his emotionless yet widening dark pupils. Yes, to him this was having sex—but to her it was making love. It always had been and always would be, she thought, wondering why it felt like a goodbye.

He stood up, kicked off the jeans and sheathed himself swiftly. His hands cupped the soft globes of her bottom and exulted in the feel of them. The gesture felt more tender to Faye than she was sure he intended, but as he turned her around to face in the opposite direction he reached forward to stroke her breasts with equally tantalising softness.

'Dante—please!'

He did not hesitate, and entered her from behind. She felt her body, tight but eager, as his strong thighs brushed against her smooth skin, wicked and yet so—so *intimate*. For didn't he realise that she would never even have the desire to act this way unless she loved him with so much of her heart that none was left to protest? He moved within her slowly to begin with, building pace, and with every thrust he claimed a little more of her soul—filling and completing her in a way she had never known she was missing until now.

Faye had lost herself every single time she and Dante had made love, but this time she was not sure she possessed even one shard of control. She was in a world other than the one inhabited by the Faye Matteson of reality, a world where dreams no longer stopped short of eluding her grasp, and she never wanted to return. She sensed him reaching the edge, but she could not hold off her own orgasm any longer as he touched her, whispering something indiscernible but fierce in Italian. And as she cried out his name she felt something else—a warmth, an opening. His own spectacular climax followed, gripping her in his rapture. But as he met his release she realised exactly what that feeling was: the splitting of his carefully applied contraception.

She heard his intake of breath, which confirmed his own recognition. As his seed spilled forth into her body she breathed deeply, not willing even to articulate the foolish dreams that were running through her mind. Dreams that belonged in the cloud-nine moment of orgasm but not a second after. For as he withdrew from her she felt swamped by the realisation that if a new life had just begun inside her, it was the last thing a man like him would want of any woman—least of all her.

The deep sigh he released seemed to say it all. It was not the satisfied exhalation that marked the beginning of their bodies returning to their usual steady breathing after making love. It was the kind of sigh that usually came just before you offered someone your condolences—like *I'm sorry to hear he passed away*. A sigh that marked the end of something. She stood up, reaching for her clothes and putting them back on in an orderly fashion, one item at a time, as if it might work as some antidote to the chaos in her mind.

'I believe there is a pill you can take, if you're concerned.'

Faye continued to straighten her dress, focusing on some inanimate object on the other side of the room, like a ballerina determined to pirouette without losing her balance, whilst his dismissive words rampaged through her heart like a tornado.

'Of course,' she replied evasively, with what she hoped was equal detachment. 'These things happen.'

He had never seemed so cold to her—never so devoid of emotion. *If you're concerned.* But in Dante's world sex had no upshot but pleasure, did it? Was this another one of those unwritten rules that his mistresses were expected to know? That if the contraception he deemed adequate happened to fail then it became their responsibility to rectify the problem? Faye felt sick at the thought.

'Ahh, I was forgetting that you are a woman of the world,' he said, as if he had just won against himself in a game of solitaire.

No, Faye thought, I'm not. And I can't pretend I am anymore.

CHAPTER NINE

'His stamina never ceases to amaze me!'

Faye smiled politely, and attempted to sip the steaming cup of espresso in a manner which suggested that her heart was not breaking in two whilst she and Elena watched the spectacle of Dante and Max. She only prayed Elena shared her brother's lack of emotional intuition. Though inwardly she doubted it were possible that anyone else on the planet could have a heart quite so impenetrable.

'Faster, faster!' Max ordered Dante as he charged at full speed around the conservatory with his three-year-old nephew on his back, their dark heads pressed together, laughing like naughty schoolboys. The irony was not lost on Faye as she watched them.

'He's been up since six.' Elena laughed, watching her son with a look of motherly adoration. 'And still such energy. Mind you, I'm not sure which one of them's encouraging the other most!'

Faye helplessly followed her gaze. This was exactly what she had been dreading, only worse. Ten times worse. Being embraced like a sister again by Elena, whom she had come to care for in her own right, and now being introduced to Max too. She had known it would be difficult, meeting another member of Dante's family as if they were in a real relationship with some kind of future, but she hadn't anticipated that he would be as sensational with children as he was with everything else he touched. Or that she would feel as if she was looking through some nightmarish kaleidoscope, where one minute he was instructing her how to be sure she was not pregnant and the next playing the family man.

'Max does seem very confident.' She turned to Elena and, remembering the way her mother had somehow gained the ability to put on a brave face at her father's funeral, forced herself to replicate it. 'I would have expected him to be more timid with an uncle he must not see very often.'

'He is very sure of himself even with strangers.' Elena nodded. 'But Dante is around more than you'd imagine. I think he's even more enamoured with his nephew than his nephew is with him.'

'I can see that.' How much easier it would have been to hear that his visits here were fleeting, to think only of the Dante who lived in that stark apartment in Rome.

'You'd like children of your own one day?' Elena's eyes followed Faye's. Dante and Max were now engaging in a particularly athletic wheelbarrow race, their faces red and full of exhilaration.

'One day, perhaps. Under the right circumstances.' Faye nodded and moved her gaze to the trees beyond the window, whose leaves were just beginning to turn brown.

'Are you not close to the right circumstances now?' Elena coaxed.

'I couldn't be further from them,' Faye replied, a little too loudly as she turned back to face her.

It was the first time Dante had looked at her since she had emerged in the living room, not long after he had answered the doorbell that had put an end to their agonising exchange. He had not batted an eyelid at her tousled hair, hastily tied back into a ponytail, nor the flush still present in her cheeks when she had excused herself for her slightly delayed entrance. No, his handling of the whole situation had been far too practised for that. But now, as Elena handed Max his juice, the look of utter disdain he aimed at her the minute his sister's attention was diverted was undeniable.

'Would you like a biscuit, Max?' Faye asked, holding out the plate, determined to distract herself.

Max gratefully accepted the proffered snack and flew from his mother's arms to place his chubby hands around Faye's neck, planting an enormous kiss on her cheek.

'Well, thank you,' Faye said playfully.

'Something tells me he's going to be a hit with the ladies,' Dante drawled.

'Just like his uncle,' Elena said instantly, but then bit her lip, as if she wished she could take the words back.

Yet Faye was numb to Elena's pained expression. Nothing she said could hurt her any more than *he* already had. Even if she had just confirmed that Faye was nothing more than one in a long line of women second only in length to the line still queuing. She knew it all already.

The room was still save for the sound of Max quietly draining his cup of juice. Elena seemed desperate to break the silence.

'So, has Dante convinced you to stay in Italy longer than just a few weeks yet, Faye? It is so easy to fall in love with it here.'

Out of the corner of her eye Faye saw Dante raise his eyebrows quizzically. What could she say? *I would stay here for the rest of my life if your brother wanted me even half as much as I want him. But I can't go on, knowing I'll never have all this, pretending it's not tearing me apart.*

'It is beautiful. But far from convincing me to stay, Dante has made me realise the necessity of keeping things varied in life.' Faye looked at him, foolishly willing him to contradict her. She'd expected him to visibly breathe a sigh of relief, but saw only condemnation in his face.

'As you can see, the fleeting nature of our arrangement suits Faye down to the ground.' He turned to Elena. 'Now, let me drive you home. It is beginning to get dark, and Max is looking tired.'

Elena stood up and wiped the blackcurrant moustache from Max's mouth, her questioning look gone in an instant, as if everything she had just heard was the most natural exchange in the world. Faye felt paralysed.

'Goodbye, Faye—and in case I don't see you before you return home, have a safe journey.' She met Faye's eyes in a look that seemed to hold a meaning Faye could not quite fathom. 'I feel sure we will meet again.'

You're wrong, Faye wanted to say. Elena's words had somehow clarified exactly what she must do to prevent any further pain. *You're wrong because I have to stop the heartache now, and I am never, never putting myself through it again.*

'Thank you for everything, Elena,' Faye said finally, kissing her on both cheeks with affection. 'And goodbye, Max. It was a pleasure to meet you.' Faye bent down to shake his tiny hot hand and lifted the corners of her mouth in what she hoped looked like a smile. But his perplexed expression as he followed his mother and uncle to the door told her she had failed.

The minute Faye heard the front door click behind them she sank to the floor like a puppet whose strings had been cut, bewildered by the events of last twenty-four hours. But what had suddenly changed? She had known all along that she was nothing more than a brief affair to him—hell, hadn't the contract set it out clearly enough? She could hardly accuse him of not being honest. No, she was the one who had changed—because she had allowed herself to *feel*, and that was precisely what she had forbidden herself to do. She had told herself she was capable of being like him, but she was as wrong now as she had been at eighteen. Only this time she couldn't pretend that she hadn't seen it coming.

And she had done it again for what? The conditional offer of money with a demand that was—when she considered it without the rose-tinted glasses she had chosen to view it through—utterly impossible to meet? She was fighting a losing battle in every corner. What would sticking around and tormenting herself for another few weeks achieve? The longer she was here, the more deeply she'd fall in love with him.

Love. She hated to admit it. It was the stupid teenager's word she had gamely attributed to her feelings for him before she'd known how foolish it was to give her heart so readily. The word she could excuse herself for thinking during sex, but which in the cold light of day simply made her feel pathetic. Yet, try as she might to use grown-up definitions like lust or chemistry, there really was no other description for the feeling in her chest when he whispered her name, when he held her in his sleep, when she watched him playing with Max. He might be incapable of anything but a temporary affair, but love didn't ask questions like *Is he suitable?* or *Will he love you back?* did it?

Which was precisely why she had to leave. For if she stayed there would only be more waking up in his arms, more admiring the way he went about his life and his work, whilst knowing just how little respect he had for her. What would he do next? Arrange a taxi to take her to the local chemist for a morning-after pill the moment he returned? Then resume their arrangement until the hour of reckoning came, when he would shake her hand to close the deal and thank her for her services? No, she couldn't bear it. She had to go.

Much as she couldn't endure the thought of returning to the restaurant she loved and watching it fall around her, nor bear to see the crushed look on her mother's face the moment she told her there was no hope, she knew if she stayed here it would destroy her. And then he would destroy Matteson's anyway. Maybe she could appeal to the banks again? There had to be something she hadn't tried, didn't there?

Although she knew in her heart the answer was no, there suddenly seemed only one way to proceed. Leave now, or break down completely. Hauling herself to her feet, she made her way to the bedroom she had not slept in since the first night she arrived and pulled her suitcase from under the bed.

Faye was packing up her toiletries in the bathroom when she heard the click of the front door again. She felt her heart sink. Not that she could have possibly hoped to vacate the villa before he returned; Elena only lived five minutes away, and the taxi Faye had ordered in her broken Italian was bound to take its time. She just had to pray that he would not attempt to halt her progress simply because her departure flouted their contract. Pray he would make this easy, agree that whatever *this* was, it had run its course.

'Going somewhere?' His tone was loaded with wry surprise as he appeared at the bathroom door, his dark figure suddenly making the room seem tiny.

'Yes. Home.'

'Really? How foolish of me to think you had signed a contract to the contrary.' His eyes bored into her. 'If this is a tantrum because I refused you your shopping trip, then save it. I'll order a car to take you wherever it is you desire.'

'That won't be necessary. I've ordered a taxi to the airport myself, thank you.' She almost felt him wince that she had dared to undermine his control. She was glad.

'Is this an attempt to get my money early, Faye? Because if so you'll be sorely disappointed. I'm afraid I *never* alter the terms of a contract.'

'I don't doubt it. And, no, believe it or not it's because I wish to go home.'

'And why might that be?' He was close behind her now, as she looked down at the cream marble floor, unable to bring herself to meet the reflection of his gaze in the mirror. 'Do not tell me it is because you have not been enjoying yourself, because I know that is not true.'

She could feel the warmth of his breath on her neck playing havoc with her insides. 'I can't do this any longer.'

'This?' His tone had the unique quality of being both deceptively soft and wholly merciless. 'Has living in luxury with every pleasure you could wish for at your fingertips in exchange for exactly what you asked me for *and* more become too much of a strain, Miss Matteson?' He stepped back, raising his eyebrows in mockery.

'I came to you about business, Dante. You were the one who insisted on treating me as your mistress.'

'How ironic, when I once brought you here for business and you insisted upon *acting* like my mistress.'

Faye wished the room would expand, or that his damn reflection didn't dominate everywhere she tried to focus.

'I was a teenager. I'd never—'

He would not let her finish. 'And what is your excuse for falling into the role so easily now?' he spat, refusing to revisit the guilt he had once felt, knowing she deserved none of it. 'Is it because you are so experienced at playing the part that it comes naturally? Maybe that is why you're walking away? Because you have found you can get your precious money in half the time by selling yourself elsewhere?'

She closed her eyes and took a step towards the door, determined to harden her heart to him for the last time. 'Like you said, this was never going to be a permanent arrangement. I'll return your initial advance. Best to leave before one of us grows tired of the other, wouldn't you say?'

If he had made just one move to stop her she would have been powerless against him, Faye thought vainly as she lugged her suitcase up the stairs to the front door of her flat in the pitch dark. The hallway light was out again. But nothing. She had expected him to call her a liar, to demand she make good on their contract—hell, even seduce her into taking it back. For heaven knows she would have succumbed. But he had stood resolutely still whilst she had walked past his hard, heartless body for the last time.

But then he'd had no reason to stop her, Faye thought wretchedly as she fumbled to find the keyhole before dragging her small suitcase in behind her. For wasn't she as easy to replace as a blown bulb? There were countless women who would no doubt be glad to share his bed, happy not to question their position in his life when it came with so many material benefits.

She turned on the light and glanced around her tiny flat, at the practical brown armchair, the putrid digits of her alarm clock flashing 12:45, and tried not to think about just how much it contrasted with where she had gone to sleep last night. The place had never looked so dreary and devoid of life. Even her answering machine winked no green light. She wondered where on earth *she* was in the boxy intersecting rooms—she who loved to contemplate design. It looked as if their occupant was someone who had spent her life living by the rules, and suddenly she hated it.

But look what happened when you followed emotions and acted impulsively, she thought. She was returning to Matteson's more in debt than when she'd left, her heart no longer whole but shattered into pieces that she couldn't put together. She stood up and moved to methodically begin her unpacking. Except she couldn't do it. For once in her life even the thought made her feel sick, as if he had rearranged the internal organs in her body and no amount of organisation could restore her to the person she had been before. Faye sat down, and for the first time in years she allowed herself to cry.

It was nausea of a very different kind which overcame her the following month as she held the white stick in her hand and closed her eyes, trying to think inconsequential thoughts the way she would if she was waiting for a bus.

And there was plenty to think about, for thinking was the one thing she had forbidden herself to do since the moment she had gone back to Matteson's the day after she had returned. Because although she had walked through the door preparing to admit defeat, the first thing she had laid her eyes upon was the initial renovation Dante's advance had set in motion: the new shop front, the first steps towards a new, improved kitchen. And though it ought to have plunged her into an even deeper pit of despair, knowing that she now owed even more money and that they could not afford to *proceed* with the plans, somehow it had had the opposite effect. For the change had made Faye instantly refocus and remember her deep-rooted passion for the business that had resurfaced in the Perfezione kitchen, and she'd suddenly felt sure that the good work that was already underway would help her cause in finding investment.

And, to her open-mouthed astonishment, she had been right. Thanks to photos of the first few renovations, and her happening to mention her recent experience abroad, the bank had actually showed real interest in her plans for the first time, rather than treating them as the naive pipedreams of an inexperienced graduate. And upon examining how, in spite of difficulties, she had now completed a year of successful mortgage repayments, *finally* the stern face of the middle-aged bank manager had softened, and he had spoken the words that were music to her ears.

'Very well, Miss Matteson, we will grant you a loan in order to cover the main improvements you propose.'

It was the break Faye needed—that Matteson's needed—and she had immersed herself in what needed to be done immediately, determined this was one opportunity that she would not let slip through her fingers. She'd taken on the young interior designer she had approached previously, keen to showcase her talents, because she was at last able to pay for the materials. She'd sent pre-designed marketing material to proper print houses, adverts to newspapers, had interviewed and appointed the restaurant manager that they hadn't previously been able to afford to replace.

The days had passed in a blur of speed as each change was completed and, thanks to her widespread publicity generating interest about their new look, the customers slowly began to trickle back. Of course it was early days, but on the face of it life *looked* more promising than it had done in years. Even if behind closed doors, when she came home to her flat at night, she forced herself to watch trashy television rather than dwell on the fact that she was eating alone. Where once she had relished her independence, now the best she could hope for was reaching for the banana she ate for dessert without wondering where *he* was eating, and with whom. With the redhead who had so closely guarded his office against female intruders, perhaps? Or skipping food altogether and lounging in the back of some taxi, making eyes as he had once made eyes at her?

And although she had promised herself she would not think about him again until after the official grand reopening next weekend, there was only so long that she could go on ignoring the more physical reminders of her time in Italy. Reminders that since returning to England it had been convenient not to consider. Like the fact that her period was late, or that she had been sick every morning for almost a week and there wasn't a bug going around.

Which brought her back to the present with a start.

When Faye opened her eyes, it felt as if she had got someone else's holiday snaps accidentally mixed up with her own. But when she shut her eyes and opened them again it was still there.

The thin blue line.

It was as if the bus she had imagined waiting for had arrived and mowed her down.

So, she thought, he *was* so damn virile that once was enough for his seed to take root in her womb and create a tiny life inside of her. *Pregnant.* She rolled the word over in her mind, as yet too strange to say aloud. She had known it was a possibility, of course, but the difference between the idea floating around in her head like a dream and the reality of the evidence before her were worlds apart. Rather like imagining she was capable of a no-strings-affair, she thought wretchedly. But as she stroked her hand over her abdomen, the thought that she was carrying *his* child felt as natural and inevitable as waking up to find it was morning. For one insane moment her eyes darted to the telephone and she envisaged dialling his number. And then she remembered how plainly he had instructed her to take a pill—how she knew within the very depths of her soul that there was nothing he would want less than this. She imagined trying to explain it to him. Surely he would want nothing to do with his child? Six years ago she would have put money on it, but now she had seen him with Max, and given what she now knew of his own childhood, she couldn't help thinking that he would be only too determined not to let history repeat itself. But wasn't it also a given that he would assume she was trying to trap him for money? The thought made her heart sink. Making that call *would* inevitably force him to re-enter her life against his wishes, because his damn traditional Italian views would make him feel duty-bound to do so. She couldn't think of anything worse.

It would be selfish not to tell him. She knew that. She owed it to their unborn child to do it. But at this moment in time, when she needed to get used to the idea herself, she couldn't. She walked across the landing to the spare bedroom, currently awash with the art materials she had used to inspire her new ideas for the restaurant, and tried to visualise it as a nursery. She could work and bring up their child here, couldn't she?

Faye drew a slow, ragged breath. It wasn't ideal, it wasn't the way she had always dreamed she would bring up a child, but she would manage. And she *would* tell him—once next weekend was out of the way, once Matteson's required less of her energy. But until then she would refrain from wondering *how* for just a few days longer.

CHAPTER TEN

HER leaving early had saved him a small fortune. Saved, too, the inevitable and troublesome exchange that came when an affair lost its spark. So why wasn't he still in Tuscany thanking his lucky stars? Or back in Rome knocking on the door of that striking French actress who had taken such pains to whisper to him exactly which room she was staying in when she had introduced herself at Il Maia last week?

His eyes rested upon the tormenting sight of Faye's bottom sashaying to and fro through the narrow sliver of glass in the kitchen door, and the blood rushing around his body filled him with anger as rapidly as it rushed to another place entirely. At first he had assumed his annoyance would pass. The way it always did on the rare occasions when a deal didn't go his way and he later discovered a better one. But as the weeks had gone by he'd been irritated to find that, on the contrary, it only grew. In fact, his frustration at the memory of that ice-maiden face of hers as she had walked away—not a *glimmer* of emotion— was surpassed only by the hot, fervid dreams that filled his nights, spilled over into his days and refused to subside.

Was it because the instant he had made up his mind that the best course of action was to return to the social scene in

Rome he had run straight into the notorious Chris and been forced to concede that he *had* been wrong on that account? Or was it just because *she* had had the audacity to end their affair before he did? Probably. After all, he couldn't remember another occasion when a woman had walked out on *him*, let alone a time when anyone had turned their back on a contract with Valenti Enterprises. Twice. Had she really supposed there would be no consequence?

Dante shifted slightly, in order to watch as a waitress whispered in her ear, and he saw her face drop instantly. Yes, he thought, allowing himself a small, throaty murmur of triumph as she slowly turned her head and he saw her eyes widen in shock, it seemed she had.

It was the worst thing she could have imagined, and the last thing she had expected—tonight. Tonight, when what she needed most was to focus on Matteson's. Faye looked reluctantly, as if she had been asked to identify a body at some horrific crime scene as the hubbub of activity in the kitchen continued around her, unprepared for the instant pang of need that ricocheted through her gut as her eyes met his. But it was not just the carnal desire that seemed to be his God-given gift to evoke in women everywhere, but a new need that was unique to her. The need to go to the father of the baby growing inside her, to have him envelop her in the protectiveness of his arms. And that was the most dangerous need she had ever known.

Her self-preservation instinct was to turn and run, never to know why the hell he was here, rather than face him. But her gut feeling was for once outweighed by something stronger. For the moment she saw him it was as if he turned the key in the ignition of her unassailable guilt, and it was gaining speed.

It was a sensation which moved her limbs before she gave them permission to walk the all too familiar gauntlet. She was pushing open the door, ignoring the dryness in her mouth, the sound of her heartbeat so loud in her ears that it drowned out the sounds of the other diners. She should have told him— had to tell him. Whatever she thought she had been doing she had simply been putting it off. She only wished she had thought about *how*.

Her stomach tied itself in knots as she reached his table. 'Dante.' Her voice was strained as she stood there, taking him in as if unable to believe he was real, not having a clue what else to say. 'What are you doing here?'

Though she had promised herself not to think of him since the night she had returned home, she realised she had pictured him so often that she knew his face off by heart. He had lost weight, fractionally. How typical that it only made his olive skin cling more closely to his chiselled jaw beneath the permanent five o'clock shadow, making him appear even more startlingly male if that was possible.

'What everyone else is doing here, I imagine. Having dinner.' The place looked good. She looked good. Too good. The way she moved around the restaurant exuded talent and an enthusiasm for the place that lingered in her wake, reminding him precisely why she had gained his respect and admiration once before, and threatened to do so all over again. But her prim black dress and her hair all pinned back from her face seemed only to reinforce that expression which said *I'm untouchable. Dio!* How tempting it was to rip the dark fabric in two right now and toss those hairpins all over the newly polished floor until she purred that she would go mad *unless* he touched her.

'I heard there had been some changes—new menu, innovative décor. It sounded—how do you say?—my cup of tea.'

Part of her wanted to blurt it out, to wipe the sardonic smile off that outrageously sensual mouth and silence his merciless repartee once and for all. The other part thanked God that she wasn't any further along, that her body at least was giving nothing away.

'And you just happened to be in England?' Her voice was hushed but insistent. Had he come to see whether she had failed as thoroughly as he had been convinced she would—in the hope that the whole evening would be a total disaster and he would be able to swipe the restaurant from under her nose?

'I never just *happen* to be anywhere, Faye. Surely you know that by now?' he chided her, clicking his tongue and making no attempt to lower his own voice. 'I have business in London.'

Faye frowned. He had no business *here*. Which was what made it all the more unnerving. Could he know? No, she hadn't told a soul. It might feel as if he was capable of reading her mind on occasions, but he wasn't psychic.

Her puzzled look irked him. 'Let me refresh your memory. Did you not sign a contract which stated that a month after you returned here I would require a cut of double your profits if you succeeded or a cut of the business if you failed?

Faye stared at him blankly, wondering if she had heard him correctly, whilst at the same time a tiny tremor of fear began to judder at the base of her spine.

'The contract is null and void, Dante. I transferred every penny you gave me right back to your account.'

'And in your eyes that constitutes the contract being null and void, does it, Miss Matteson? Clearly we didn't spend long enough studying the legal side of running a successful business.' Patronisingly, he shook his head and tutted. 'Oh, wait—that was due to be covered at the *end* of the month. I seem to recall you took the decision not to see your side of the contract through and stay until that point. Regrettable, you might say.'

Faye's face fell, but she stood her ground. She had worked too hard.

'I owe you nothing. The cash has been repaid.'

Though she had dared to believe that Matteson's takings were slowly beginning to improve, any profit was being ploughed back into the business, into repaying the bank. Even if she did owe him a penny—which she didn't—she had none to give.

'But what about repayment for the *skills* you acquired under my tuition? You are making a profit, yes? Do not stand before me and pretend *experience* means so little to you.'

The sensual drawl of his voice seemed to reach into Faye and tweak every nerve-ending in her body. She began to shiver, but tensed her shoulders to counteract it, determined not to let him see.

'If you had taken the time to read my proposal you would know that every change I have made here was based on plans I created before I even arrived in Rome.' It was true. Yes, she might have rediscovered her passion for the business in Italy, but the ideas for here were hers alone.

'So what was it that persuaded the bank to loan you the money, *cara*, given that nothing had changed? Could it have been perhaps that they saw from your account that *I* had been willing to invest? Did you inform them you had undergone a period of learning alongside me?'

Colour shot hotly through her cheeks. She was furious that

she was even wondering whether his words held any element of truth. The bank had finally agreed because she had kept up her repayments, because they saw potential—hadn't they?

She looked at the way he was lounged back in his chair, with the river outside the window behind him, as if he was king of the whole bloody world—whilst she stood there like some minion who had been summoned for his amusement once more. Wasn't it about time he learned that the world turned of its own accord, without him twirling it? Yes, it might always be in the shade when he wasn't there, but that was beside the point.

'The thought of a woman making her own way in this world really gets to you, doesn't it, Dante?'

'Still such fire, Faye. You know, if you are unable to come up with the cash there may be another way to see the contract through to a mutually satisfying conclusion.' His eyes licked over her, sensual promise written all over his face. 'How about I take you for a drink when you're finished here. Toast your success?'

It was more than she could bear. He had played with her as a tomcat tormented a mouse, and now he was back for the kill. And for no other reason than that the sport amused him. It was time.

'I'm afraid that won't be possible, Dante.'

'And why might that be, when every inch of your body is craving my touch, right here, right now, even in this public restaurant?'

'Because I'm pregnant.'

Faye would have laughed and made a mental note to write that one down as the all-time greatest conversation-stopper if it hadn't been true—if the look on his face hadn't been everything she had feared. It hardly mattered that she hadn't allowed herself to think about how to say it or when, because even if she *had* thought about nothing else she would have known it was always going to be this hideous, regardless of whether she built up to it slowly or blurted it out so spectacularly.

For once in his life Dante was still, his face creased in such disbelief that she might as well have just revealed that she was extra-terrestrial.

'How is this possible?'

She wanted to patronisingly deliver a concise biology lesson, to point out that nature had invented sex with a greater goal than his pleasure, but his voice had lost its cut-glass quality, his Italian accent was stronger than ever, and instinctively she knew it would be the wrong thing to do.

'This pill—it did not work?'

Faye drew in a deep breath. 'I couldn't—no.'

He raised his head then, the look of bewilderment that had been aimed nowhere in particular suddenly directed unequivocally at her.

'Couldn't?'

'It was not something I wished to do.'

'In the same way as *telling me* was not something you wished to do?' His sardonic tone was back, the stillness it had been so rare to witness in him replaced by movement as he threw one leg over the other. 'How long have you known?'

'Only a week—for certain.' She wished it did not sound so predictable, so *pathetic*. 'I was going to tell you.'

'When?' he questioned accusingly, drumming two long fingers on the table. 'When it suited you to milk the benefits of my paternity at some later date? Save yourself for one lump sum?'

'I want nothing from you, Dante. I can raise this child alone.'

He stood up immediately, his full height beside her slender frame never so striking.

'Alone? You are suggesting that you would raise this child without him even being aware of his father, his Italian heritage?' he boomed, so that several diners turned around, before politely looking back at their meals and pretending they had seen nothing out of the ordinary. 'If you even *try*, I will fight you every step of the way.'

The trembling that had begun at the base of her spine spread through her limbs as the full weight of his threat seeped into her. The most dangerous implication of telling him hadn't occurred to her before. Now it was blindingly obvious. He had the power to extradite her from their child's life completely.

'But this is hardly the place to discuss the legalities,' he continued brusquely, as a sheepish-looking waitress hesitated at Faye's side before placing Dante's meal before him. 'I will wait for you to finish here.'

Faye barely registered the words that followed his threat, only hearing her cue to escape this intoxicating battleground she had walked into unarmed. For as she reluctantly nodded in response to his request—no, his demand to continue the conversation that she never had wanted to have, she felt as if up until that point she had been standing on a rug that had been slipping from under her so slowly she had barely noticed. Now he had torn it away in one single stroke.

He wanted their child and he would show her no mercy.

'You look like you've seen a ghost.'

Her mother was on the other side of the kitchen door, the

delight that had lit her face at the start of tonight's grand re-opening now replaced with concern.

Faye breathed weakly as Josie Matteson looked past her and out across the tables. She didn't doubt news of the striking Italian seated at the best table in the house had already done the rounds.

'Signor Valenti is here because he regrets not continuing his involvement, perhaps?' Josie questioned softly.

Faye shook her head dejectedly. 'The multimillion-dollar profits from his own restaurants ensure regret is not an emotion he need trouble himself with, Mum.'

Josie took hold of her arm, sensing her fragility, and moved them both out of the thoroughfare of the waitresses before turning to face her.

'I wasn't talking about the restaurant.'

Faye raised her head, blinking first in astonishment and then to stop the tears which threatened to fall. Her mother swept the strand of hair that had fallen across Faye's eyes to one side.

'It makes no difference.' Faye shrugged. Matteson's, her, the baby. Dante built his success out of having no regrets, working every situation to his advantage.

'And yet he is here, looking at you like I have only ever seen one other man look at a woman—'

'No,' Faye protested helplessly.

'The way your father used to look at me,' Josie continued.

'He's nothing like Dad.' The speed of her rejoinder was more revealing than she knew.

Josie sighed. 'Your father would have been very proud of you tonight, Faye. *I'm* proud.'

'I only did what needed to be done.'

'It is no small achievement,' Josie said calmly, in the voice of a mother who understood that at times her daughter was her own worst enemy. 'But what about what you need to do for yourself, Faye?'

Faye frowned, fearing she had made it sound as if this had only been about doing her daughterly duty. 'I didn't mean—'

'I know you didn't, and I know you love this business, but Matteson's itself was your father's dream. That was why he never wanted you to give up your studies. He wanted you to find something that made you as happy as you were the day you got offered the job in Rome.' She smiled slowly and kissed Faye's cheek. 'It's time to live your own dreams.'

If only it was that simple, Faye thought. If only she could have breezed through the unmitigated success of this evening believing that Dante was waiting in the wings to realise her dreams for her. But whatever Josie thought she had read in his eyes, the meaning of his words the minute he had discovered her pregnancy had been unequivocal. *I'll fight you every step of the way.*

That was all that lay ahead—the only vision in her mind as she plastered on an aching smile that belied the anguish of her heart, clinging to the futile hope that if she stayed here late enough he might grow tired of waiting for her to leave, and she might not have to face the words she dreaded tonight.

She shook her head at the other staff as they entreated her to go home. Found a million jobs to occupy her time. But as she locked up and wound her chunky knitted scarf around her neck against the cold bite of the late-October night, unable to stretch out the evening any longer, she saw it immediately. The sleek, low-slung vehicle on the opposite side of the street. Affluent though this neighbourhood was, there could be no pretending, even through the hazy streetlights, that it was the kind of model your average wealthy businessman would drive. It was in a class of its own.

'Do not tell me that your usual method of transport at this hour is on foot?' His incredulous voice cut through the half-open tinted window, penetrating the darkness.

Faye froze on the pavement. 'I only live a few streets away.'

'That doesn't make it any more acceptable. You're a woman. You should not walk alone in the middle of the night.'

'Yes, well, we're not all billionaires.'

'And we're not all pregnant either.' He said the word as if it was new, unfamiliar. 'Now, get in.'

Faye walked over to the car, irked to find herself grateful that she did not have to walk. The exhaustion of the day's events and the tiredness of being pregnant were beginning to catch up with her.

'I'm having a baby. I'm not terminally ill,' she ground out as he held open the door for her. She sank into the luxurious heated leather seat, the weariness in her limbs seeping away, though she couldn't help feeling this mode of transport couldn't be any more different from the carefree motorbike he had driven in another place, in what felt like a different lifetime.

'Which is why you *should* be taking the utmost care of yourself.' His voice was laced with both anger and concern. For *his* child? she wondered. A pity he had been devoid of such humanity when he had told her to take a pill, or demanded she become his mistress for a month and then repay him over the odds for the experience.

'I have profits to double—remember?'

But he ignored her, as if in his mind she had slipped into

a new female role because of her *condition*. From fallen woman to vessel carrying his child, she thought.

Dante crunched the gears, his frustration evident as he swung the car lithely around the end of the street in response to her directions. How crazy it was that there were so many day-to-day details about each other's lives that they didn't know—like something as simple as where she lived. No doubt that was precisely why affairs suited him: all the benefits of a relationship but none of the banalities a man who was head of an international empire wouldn't have the time or the inclination to learn.

'Doubling your profits, or should I say *attempting* to double your profits, will no longer be necessary.' His words were delayed, his voice reluctant, like a football manager forced to retract a boast after losing at home.

'Necessary for whom?' she asked, maddened by his pronouncement. 'Believe it or not seeing Matteson's do well again has always been *my* priority—even if it doesn't matter to you.'

'You cannot seriously be suggesting that you would carry on working these hours with a child?'

'Why not? It *is* possible for a woman to juggle the responsibilities of a career and a family, you know.' In an ideal world she would like nothing more than to raise their child without the pressures of work, to give their child the idyllic upbringing she had been lucky enough to experience. But life didn't always turn out the way you wanted it to.

'Juggle?' He spat out the word in distaste, raking his hand through his hair. 'Pass my child from pillar to post whilst you focus on your *career*, as if my child is some raggy doll?'

'Rag doll,' Faye corrected, and would have smiled in any other situation at how endearing it was on the rare occasions when English phrases eluded him. Would have if they had not been fighting over the one thing that ought to bond a man and woman inseparably together, but which only seemed to be driving them further and further apart.

'You will not need to juggle anything. I will see to that.'

So now he would *gladly* throw money at her? 'And what if I *wish* to continue working?'

'No child of mine will come second to the wishes of his mother.'

His, Faye noted, and not for the first time. Of course he would presume it was a boy. But then she looked into his eyes and saw something of the little boy he had once been, the little boy who had come second to *his* mother's wishes, and for one insane moment she wanted to reach across and obliterate that look on his face with a kiss.

But as Dante drew up outside her block of flats and killed the engine, she felt only a chill where there had once been fire. No, whatever passion there had once been on his part seemed to have died the moment she had confessed—to what she supposed in his eyes was a mistress's ultimate transgression.

'Thank you for the lift,' she said meekly, raising her hand to the handle on the car door, hoping that somehow this would be the end of it. Praying that whatever demand he had hinted at earlier would keep for another day, when she was stronger, when maybe *she* might have built up some immunity to him.

But he was ignoring her. 'This—' he stared grimly out of the car window '—is where you propose to raise my child?'

Faye followed his gaze, seeing it in the way he must see it instead of as the adequate, functional place she had chosen to rent after uni, when she had first come back to Matteson's. It was true that the antiquated block looked a little as if it could model for a cover shot of Dickens' *Bleak House*, but it was the middle of the night, on a cold autumnal evening in the suburbs. And it was starting to rain. What did he expect? To drive round the corner and find a spacious family home akin to his villa in Tuscany, miraculously bathed in the golden glow of sunshine? No, of course he didn't, and that was precisely his point.

'It's better than it looks,' she threw out defensively, her hand still resting on the door handle. 'And anyway, I don't consider it matters *where* a child is brought up, so long as it is loved.'

'No? You suppose that being an illegitimate child, brought up by a mother working full-time to pay the bills, is an ideal start in life?'

Faye noticed the way he visibly blanched at the word *illegitimate*. Yes, she had always imagined that if she were ever blessed with children she would be married, but considering *he* was supposed to thrive on adapting to change his views were immovable!

'Not ideal, no. But better than being torn between two parents caught in some hideous legal battle.'

'My thoughts exactly, *cara*,' he said slowly, his eyes glittering.

Faye looked at him in the light of the dim streetlamp, perplexed as much by the look on his face as by the words he had spoken.

'Then what do you propose, Dante?'

'That you become my wife.'

CHAPTER ELEVEN

No, Faye thought, that's not a proposal at all. You're inform-ing me that this is how it's going to be. As if I'm some newly discovered supplier for your business whose goods you want to buy, so you're blinding me with an offer beyond my wildest dreams without even considering what that might do to me.

She stared at him, searching his face without knowing what she expected to find there, as the rain beat down harder upon the windscreen. There *was* nothing to find there. She was pregnant with his child so he felt duty-bound to wed her, to ensure that the heir to Valenti Enterprises was legitimate, to make sure the mother of his child did nothing so crassly inappropriate as work for a living. Nothing else.

Against her will, an image of the villa in Tuscany entered her mind unbidden, of herself standing at the door waiting with their child as Dante came home to them. It caused some-thing deep within her to blossom. No, she told herself, it would be nothing like that. Because *that* picture of marriage was filled with love, and his *proposal* was about anything but that. And suddenly the daydream changed into a nightmare. Their child tucked up in bed whilst she waited for him, not knowing where he was or who he was with, only knowing that she was expected to turn a blind eye. And how could she live alongside him, loving without reciprocation, when even just one week in Italy had almost broken her?

'You consider it a necessity for a mother and father who do not love one another to suffer living together for the sake of their child?' Faye asked.

His mouth hardened. For one tiny moment Faye felt a tiny surge of triumph amidst all the pain. She could just imagine the way Dante would have envisaged a woman replying to the offer of becoming Mrs Valenti, and it would be nothing like the response she had just uttered.

'I doubt the odds of our being able to bear living with one another are any worse than any other couple's,' he shot out, his vexation tangible. He raised one eyebrow sardonically. 'At least we already know we are compatible in the bedroom.'

Faye looked at him dismally. For where would she be left when he grew bored with her, as he inevitably would? 'There is more to a marriage than sex, Dante.'

He felt a surge of frustration. She dismissed her desire for him as if it was nothing more than a memory she had taped up in a box and left in baggage reclaim! How satisfying it would be to run his hands over that soft and supple body beneath that oh-so-functional coat and feel her infused with so much heat that she would be unable to think of anything but making love to him. Yet for once in his life there was something else he wanted more.

'Yes, there is more to a marriage than having sex,' he ground out, determined to dampen his own insistent desire. 'Like having children.'

What about love? Faye's heart screamed. Doesn't that enter this impossible equation?

'Plenty of people have children *without* being married. What if I wish to stay here?' The rain was lashing down so hard now that her block of flats was barely visible. Why was it she always seemed to end up arguing for that which was furthest from what she actually wanted when it came to Dante? How was she even pretending that *here* was a better alternative? Because she had her own pride, she thought brokenly, her own dreams.

'Why? Because you would have your freedom?' His voice was clipped as he turned away from her, disgust written all over his face.

'Because I'm needed at Matteson's.' Funny how arguments like *this is my home*, or *maybe I hope to one day find a man who'll love me back* didn't even enter her head. Because there had only been once in her life when she had felt as if she had really belonged somewhere, or truly loved someone, and it hadn't been here.

'I was impressed tonight,' he said frankly. It caused a swelling of pride deep within her. 'Money need no longer be a concern. I see no reason not to release you from your commitment to the bank and invest myself.'

It ought to have been her moment of sheer triumph, of proving him wrong, but it had come too late. He had believed she deserved nothing, and now he was throwing money at her for no other reason than to get to his baby. And yet she couldn't deny that he was making accepting his marriage demand seem feasible, doable.

'You can continue with the design side of the business from abroad, if necessary.'

'You wouldn't *rather* I stay here? Have your lawyers fight me for full custody?' She was daring to play devil's advocate with a scenario that made her stomach feel as if she had done ten rounds in a boxing ring, but she needed to understand.

'I believe a child needs his mother.'

His decision made sense. Deep down she believed a child needed its father in equal measure. But he couldn't have spelled out more clearly that her role would effectively be that of biological nanny. The thought made her chest ache.

He grew impatient at her silence. 'But if this is to be your answer then you leave me little choice but to take legal action.'

Faye felt the blood drain from her face. She was silent for a long moment, knowing this was the hour of reckoning, that she had a split second to make her choice. Except there wasn't really a choice to make, was there? How could there be?

'No, Dante, that is not my answer. Yes, I'll marry you.'

She had never imagined that she would say those words and in her heart feel anything other than the promise of sunshine. But as he saw her to the door under an enormous umbrella she wondered why he was bothering to shelter her from the rain when she felt as if it was destined to be forever winter in her heart. For he had made his offer as coolly as if it were a business takeover, and she knew the only way to survive was to match his coldness in equal measure.

'You have seen a doctor?' Suddenly it felt as if the door had been closed on any exchange other than practical details for evermore.

Faye shook her head.

'No?'

'I took a home test. I haven't had time.'

'Then we will go first thing tomorrow morning.'

Of course, Faye thought. He wants conclusive proof before he parts with any cash or even gets close to making this legal.

Never mind that I've got every physical symptom in the book. She doubted he would be convinced by something as flighty as the rhythms of her body; he had made it perfectly clear what he thought of women succumbing to those before.

'I'll book an appointment, though I doubt I'll get one straight away,' Faye said, searching for her keys. 'I'm due at the restaurant from late morning onwards as it is.'

'Matteson's will cope without you, Faye. I'll see to it.'

Two months ago she would have done anything to know that Matteson's was finally safe. Now it just felt as if she had handed him another piece of her soul.

'And as for a doctor—I'll inform the London practice of the private clinic I use that we will be arriving just after nine.'

Of course. His was a world in which people waited for *him*.

'We'll head to a jeweller afterwards. The press will no doubt expect you to be sporting a ring of epic proportions when I make the announcement.' He looked at her scathingly, as if waiting for some reaction, but her face was stony.

She had forgotten the media circus that would be bound to surround them, but suddenly it paled into insignificance as the true reality of her decision slammed into her. She remembered how, returning to her flat a month ago, she had hated just how little she seemed to have stamped her own personality on her living space. And now look at the future ahead of her: her life from now on was to be guided by where he wanted her to be and when, living up to what people expected of the wife of Dante Valenti and of the mother of his child. Never mind living space. There would be no space for *her* to have a personality what-soever. No, but she would have her baby—would wake every day no longer eaten up inside because she missed him so much that it felt as if one day the pain would stop her waking up at all.

'Very well,' she said, the realisation suddenly making compliance easy. 'See you at nine.'

But life, Faye was about to discover, was never so easy that the moment you resigned yourself to the path ahead you could just get on with walking it. Because the minute she opened her eyes the following morning she knew something wasn't right. No, something was very *wrong*. Instinctively she sat up in bed. The objects in the room came into focus though she did not really *see* any of them. It was not nausea. She found the carpet with one bare foot. It was not the unpleasant but reassuring sickness to which she had been growing accustomed. It was something else.

She stumbled to the bathroom through the half light, willing her sense of foreboding to be nothing more than the remains of last night's exchange with Dante. But the moment she stood up she felt it: the slightly damp sensation that ought to have been impossible.

Because she was pregnant, a voice screamed inside her head as she screwed up her eyes tightly and felt the coldness of the white tiles beneath her feet as she reached the bathroom. Because her last period had been weeks ago. Because her body had been telling her for days and the test had confirmed it. Which meant if—

Faye crumpled like an inflatable doll which had been pricked with a pin the minute she saw it. The dark red stain. And suddenly it felt as if she was falling from a very high building as everything she held dear was left at the top. Then everything went black.

* * *

Dante gave up pressing the bell, doubting its operation, and let himself through the inadequate security door that led into the block of twelve flats. The place did look marginally more tolerable this morning, but maybe that was because he no longer had to imagine Faye attempting to remain here and bring up their child.

Except last night could not have felt less of a victory. He had wanted her to acquiesce, of course, to admit that it made perfect sense. And he had not supposed for a minute that she wouldn't put up a fight—she was too goddamned independent not to. But did her submission have to be so cold? He had always thought he would admire detachment in a woman, so why did it make him feel as if he was doing her a wrong, trapping her when he had just promised her everything? Hell, she had played the martyr so well it had even made him think better of proving her wrong about the importance of sex when that had been his whole reason for coming here in the first place—hadn't it?

Dante took the stairs two at a time. No doubt she would come round when they swapped Harley Street for Bond Street later. Even if she had barely seemed to bat an eyelid at the prospect last night.

He had knocked three times without an answer when he began to suspect that something was wrong. She might be defiant, but this morning was about the baby, and the minute she had dropped the bombshell of her pregnancy he had witnessed within her a motherly instinct he never would have anticipated. He didn't doubt her promise that she would be here for a second.

'Faye?' he bellowed through the thin wooden door, assessing its weight with his fingertips. There was no answer. It had one catch. If needed, he could force it easily. 'Faye?'

And then he heard it. A low moan that sounded like an animal in pain.

He was inside the flat in an instant, the full force of his shoulder more than enough to break the bolt. He took in the layout of the sitting room quickly. Empty. One doorway led to what he could see was the kitchen, another to what he presumed must be the bedroom and bathroom.

'Faye!'

Faye drifted in and out of delirium as if she was watching the scene from above, observing the pitiful collection of shivering limbs and pyjamas piled on the floor as if that was all that remained of her. Somewhere in a world she was unable to identify as the one in which she was existing she heard a vague knocking, and then the calling of her name.

'*Dio*! What's the matter—the baby?'

His voice was urgent, his dark presence in the cool white room unfathomable as he got to his knees beside her, the uncharacteristic gesture only adding to her bewilderment.

Faye made another noise that seemed to come from deep within, her agony so palpable it was like smoke pervading the air.

'We're going to the hospital. Now.'

The minute he said the words, suddenly, like a blinding light, Dante felt all the fear of powerlessness coursing through his veins. And with it came the startling realisation that he had broken the rule of detachment by which he lived his life. But if it caused him to forget to take breath for a second, in the next instant his hands were scooping her up, raising her limp body into his arms.

The sensation of his warm hands against her own clammy, pallid skin shocked her into consciousness. 'No.' She shook her head from side to side, as if the action took every remaining atom of energy within her. 'The baby is…gone.'

The minute the word was out she felt the tears she had been too stunned to release begin to roll in great beads down her face.

'There's no need,' she said helplessly. 'Go—you're free now.'

'I'm not going anywhere.'

Dante felt something twist in his gut, as if he had just looked down and realised he had been crushing a small bird in the palm of his hand, and that he needed to set it free as much as it longed to fly. Throwing his grey cashmere coat round her trembling body, he kicked open every door on the way to his car, laying her gently down upon the back seat before flying behind the wheel and starting the engine.

It was the local hospital she knew: the one where she had been born, had had her tonsils removed as a girl. She supposed it ought to have been comforting. No Harley Street clinic now, for what a leveller the failure of the human body really proved to be, she thought absently, as Dante insisted she sit in a wheelchair whilst he pushed her to the relevant department. All around them were husbands pushing wives, wives pushing husbands, children pushing parents and vice versa. Everyone was being pushed by someone who cared about them.

Except they would all go on caring after they had exited through those same doors. But Dante? Could she bear to have the doctor confirm what she already knew? Have him take her home and with a pitying look break off their engagement now that the one thing that had given him reason to be here had failed to exist? It felt as if in the space of twenty-four hours fate had served up every dream she had ever had, like delicious fruits, and then left her alone to discover that every one was poisoned.

'Dante, I can't,' Faye sobbed. 'Please, let me go home.'

'No, Faye.' His voice was firm, but filled with a tenderness she barely recognised. 'I can't do that.'

For once in her life she understood that there was a time to let someone else take the reins, and that time was now.

It was the longest thirty minutes of her life. She did not know what the medics were doing, only that Dante had demanded they were seen immediately and of course he had been obeyed. Now they were checking her from head to toe, as she lay back with her eyes closed, praying that it would all soon be over. Dante never left her side—against the doctor's recommendation that he wait outside. And, regrettably, it was now that she appreciated more strongly than ever before that Dante was the man she truly loved.

Not because when he spoke she never wanted to stop listening, or because when they made love she never wanted it to end, but because he was the man she wanted with her when she was in need. She'd thought she had built her life up so independently that she didn't *need* anyone, but she needed him. And not just because he had carried her here, or had demanded that she be seen immediately. But because somehow, in this terrifying moment when she thought she was losing everything, his very presence gave her more strength than she could possibly possess alone. Yet, paradoxically, it was as if she had never been joined to him by anything more substantial than a length of cotton, and now it had grown as fine as a spider's web that any second would break. And with it the baby she had dreamed of and the man she loved would be gone, like a change in the wind, as if to all the world but her the web had never existed at all.

'Well, Faye.'

She opened her eyes and raised her hand to wipe away the tears, shaken from her semi-conscious state by the first words to have been aimed at her for what felt like an age. She shuffled up on the bed slightly, to take in the benign face of the doctor as she tried to paste on the mask of someone who could cope.

'I apologise for all the examinations, but I'm afraid it is something you are going to have to get used to.'

Faye frowned and instinctively looked to Dante. The lines she now realised had been furrowing his brow were somehow more apparent for their absence.

The doctor continued. 'A bleed in the first trimester of pregnancy is, unfortunately for the stress levels of a new mother and father, quite common. But if you look at the screen before you you will see the beginnings of your perfectly healthy baby.'

Faye suddenly registered the small monitor at the end of the bed and stared at it open-mouthed, the doctor's words still lying on the surface of her mind like precious droplets she didn't dare allow her brain to absorb.

And then she saw it. Amidst the black-and-white grains a small, perfectly formed dark shape, and the tiny beat of a heart she could just make out. To anyone else it would have looked like nothing. To Faye it was like the greatest gift she had ever been given—an artistic masterpiece that evoked within her an emotion that transcended everything else she had ever known. Her heart seemed to swell in her chest.

'Everything is OK?' Faye said, as if testing the words, still unable to believe the sight before her wasn't some mirage her mind had conjured up to protect her heart. Unconsciously she reached out her hand to Dante, resting it upon his as he stared at the screen, equally humbled and lost in his own thoughts.

The doctor smiled. 'Everything is fine. You are free to go. I recommend you refrain from work for a few days, but we won't need to see you again until your next scan at around twelve weeks.'

'Thank you.' Faye smiled at him and Dante silently shook his hand before the doctor disappeared back into the busy ward, leaving them alone.

It was then that the relief truly hit her. Relief, and a joy so impossible to contain that she forgot her pact with herself and allowed the dam that was keeping her emotions at bay to burst its banks. Their baby was OK. This was normal. She had seen it with her own eyes. As she would see it again at twelve weeks—seven weeks from now. Would she be on Italian soil? Married even?

She looked at Dante, unusually still. He might be a man whose heart was as impenetrable as a fortress, but there was no denying that he had been moved by the tiny dot on the screen before them. Faye worked her way off the bed, with his help, and hugged his jacket around her.

'Well, it looks like the ring will have to wait, I suppose,' she said lightly as they made their way towards the door, attempting to disperse some of the intensity of the moment that had caught them both unawares.

There was a time when her comment would have struck him as being the words of a true gold-digger, but that moment was past. Now it seemed only to reinforce every wrong move he had made since the minute he had returned—how irreconcilable their two worlds really were, despite the fact that they had collided to create that tiny shape on screen that had made his heart turn over like nothing else ever had.

'That won't be necessary.'

For one second Faye stupidly wondered if he was about to whip out some symbolic gem from his pocket and place it on her finger, the way they did in the movies. But she had made the mistake of believing him to be a romantic hero long ago. She shouldn't have needed to see the grim set of his side profile to know that this was no fairy tale.

'Today has made me think about what you said.'

It was the kind of sentence Dante never uttered—one in which he admitted to seeing her point of view—and yet she had never heard him sound more resolute.

'And I agree. Two parents marrying for the sake of their child is not necessarily the best option.'

Faye stopped in her tracks as they reached the corridor, to check she had heard correctly. And when she couldn't rearrange the sounds in her mind to make a sentence any more palatable she shut her eyes, praying life had an 'undo' button—like when you made a mistake on a computer and you could take away the last thing that had happened as if it had never been. But as she looked into his face she was forced to confront that it didn't. She had never seen his angular features look so *closed*; the knowledge that this was truly the end had never felt more real. As real as the baby inside her. And yet it was over anyway. The spider's web had snapped, and never in her twenty-four years had she felt so debilitated that there weren't even words.

'What about what *you* believe,' she whispered helplessly. 'About a child needing both parents?'

'I changed my mind.'

CHAPTER TWELVE

HE HAD changed his mind: of course he had. The way he changed everything. What did it matter whether the consequence was a new colour scheme at Il Maia, or her future torn apart by what might have been?

Faye sat curled on the sofa in her flat, going over the events of two days ago for what must have been the hundredth time. What *could* she have said in return? She had been the one trying to persuade him to alter his dated views on child-rearing only hours before, desperate for some alternative to spending her life living alongside a man who would never love her. She couldn't exactly turn around and beg him to marry her now, when the minute he had been forced to confront the reality of what being her husband might entail he had blatantly wanted to run a mile. Telling him would have only made him want to run farther.

Yet it wasn't as if he had done the age-old male bunk when faced with the evidence of her pregnancy. No, after casually announcing that there would be no marriage he had helped her to the car, escorted her home, insisted she rest—in fact he had acted like the perfect gentleman. He had even called yesterday morning to check she was OK. But she couldn't help wishing that he hadn't been a perfect gentleman at all. At least when she had been his mistress she had felt wanted, if only physically. Now it felt like any concern for her well-being was simply because his child was growing inside her—rather like checking that his oven was on at the right temperature.

If she hadn't been so dazed after the frightening events of that morning she might have immediately assumed that he was sweetening her up prior to commencing his custody battle after the birth. But he had even been keen to clarify that *that* was not his intention.

'We will discuss the future at another time,' he had said as he left. 'But I am sure we can come to some mutually convenient arrangement between us.'

And, though she knew he was ruthless, she also knew that dishonesty simply wasn't his style.

Which meant what, exactly? That she would be stuck in the limbo of *afterwards* for evermore? That her involvement with Dante from now on would be nothing more than stilted conversations and endless details, starting with the dates of scans until her calendar became marked with when she was to hand her child over to him, and then he back to her. She would go on loving him helplessly whilst he got on with his life, and she who had once tried so hard to bury her memories would have no hope of ever doing so. Because every time she looked at their baby she would see him. Somehow, it felt as if it would almost have been easier to fight him. It seemed preferable to facing a lifetime of his indifference.

Faye put down her pencils and looked at the sketchpad resting on her lap, all energy drained from her. She wasn't used to the rest the doctor had recommended, and which Dante had been adamant she adhere to, and she had intended to pass the time by planning a design for the spare bedroom that would become a nursery, working out where she would fit all the bits and pieces a baby would need. Except as her mind wandered she had ended up sketching an idea for a fresco—all orangey sunshine and ripe fruit trees and farm animals. The perfect scene for the wall in a bedroom in a farm-house in Tuscany. Too big and too vivid for the greying space she had here.

She closed her eyes, feeling her throat tighten. What a blessing it had been, she thought, when she had first left Italy and had been able to throw herself into work—too busy to have moments like these, when she realised that dreams she'd never meant even to have had ingrained themselves so deeply in her soul. Now she didn't even have the luxury of losing herself in Matteson's. Because even if Dante allowed her to go back she knew that over time it would require her presence less and less; the newly appointed restaurant manager looked as promising as their takings, and she could pretty much do the marketing from home.

She supposed she ought to have felt as if a great weight had been lifted from her shoulders, but she didn't. She was truly glad, of course, to see the tables full of smiling diners once more, to see employees full of new enthusiasm and no longer fearing for their jobs. To know her family's business was restored. But the events of the last few days had forced her to confront the fact that there was something even more impor-tant to her.

Because from the second she had thought she might be losing her baby she had experienced a sense of both terror and clarity unlike anything she had never known. Most immedi-ate—like being forced under water—had been the fear that this child growing inside her, for which she already felt so much love, would never have its own chance at life, or become a part of hers. Secondly, like the crest of a wave crashing down upon her, had come the fear that in losing this baby she would also lose the person she cared for the most in this world. *And* it was out of her control. She had suddenly realised that twice before *she* had brought about her separation from Dante, by walking away rather than daring to take a chance and tell him how she felt. Yes, maybe it was what he had wanted, but she had never said aloud that she couldn't continue as his mistress because he meant too much to her, or that she'd given him her virginity not because she was the harlot he supposed but because she had fallen in love with him and in her naivety had thought he might be capable of falling in love with her. The thought had made her realise that maybe she ought to have done things differently—maybe she shouldn't have tried so hard to protect her own heart. For hadn't she failed anyway?

Except what had followed was the discovery that her moment of lucidity had coincided with his—at the opposite end of the spectrum. Had it been finding her on the floor like that which had made him realise he couldn't spend his life caring for a woman he didn't love? Or seeing his baby's heart beating that had made him aware of his haste, aware that putting his fiercely traditional views into practice was going to involve a lot more than he had thought? Whatever it was, she had never known so indisputably that he did not want her to be a part of his life. And suddenly it seemed nothing good would ever come of telling him that for her the opposite was true.

She couldn't blame him, of course. He had taken the steps to ensure she never got pregnant, and he had never been anything but honest about what she was to him: first his employee, then his mistress. She had failed on both counts. She couldn't even be angry anymore. He was the man he was. The man she loved as much in spite of his frankness as because of it.

Faye was grateful that at that instant the doorbell rang, interrupting her wretched thoughts. Why did no one warn you that the aftermath of a storm could leave the heart even more desolate than when it was being beaten by the wind and the rain? Wearily, she placed her slippered feet on the floor and moved towards the door, hoping that it was someone from Matteson's, come to tell her they couldn't manage without her after all.

'Oh! It's you.'

It was ridiculous to be so surprised at the sight of him. He had said they would have to discuss details, and he had made it clear that he intended to check up on her. But as she looked at him standing there, the pale shirt open at the neck beneath his dark suit telling her this was nothing but a brief visit in between business meetings, she felt shaken nevertheless. Would she still get this preposterous whoosh of excitement ten years from now, when she sat beside him at a parents' evening listening to how their child was doing, whilst all the time she was thinking about what *she* longed to be doing with him, wondering who he was currently doing it with? Faye shook herself.

'May I come in?'

It was tempting to say no—her flat was free of him. If he came in again, then every time she looked around she would imagine the incongruous image of his dark, powerful frame dominating the small room. But hell, it was swimming before her eyes most of the time anyway.

She nodded and stepped backwards to allow him to pass her, suddenly cringing at her tasteless slippers—a gift from Chris years before, emblazoned with the word *Tart* and depicting a large cherry-topped confection. She placed one foot on top of the other.

'Coffee?' she asked, closing the door behind him and swivelling round to face him, desperate to busy her hands.

'I'll make it. Sit down,' he commanded, frowning, as if she shouldn't even be standing up—as if she should have used nothing less than telekinesis to open the door.

'No, Dante. I'll make it.'

She walked through to the kitchen, wishing she could resist snatching a glance at herself in the mirror on the way, but failing. Once out of sight, she kicked her slippers under the radiator and loosened her hair. There was little she could do about the oversized grey jumper and faded jeans. Were his women usually pampered and preened on the off-chance he might drop in? Probably, she thought. Which is precisely why *one of his women* isn't a definition that will ever apply to you again.

'I've only got instant, I'm afraid,' she called, wishing that kettles whistled as they'd used to, in order to fill the void.

'Sorry?'

She stuck her head round the door to the living room. 'Instant decaffeinated coffee, Dante, as opposed to hand-blended latte. Will that do?'

'That will be fine, thank you.'

Would she have to explain to him what a state school was, too? Or a packed lunch? No, she thought. I doubt he'll give me the chance.

He was standing by her second-hand sofa, examining the sketchpad that she had left open on the coffee table. She paused at the door, mugs in hand, wishing she had had the foresight to put it away.

'Are you feeling better?'

No, Faye thought, I'm not. *Because you're here when I know you'd rather be anywhere else.*

'A little, thank you.' She motioned to the sofa. 'Please, sit.' How had she got to this point? Where she was incapable of anything but small talk with the man she loved, the man whose child was growing in her belly, as if he was nothing more than a guest she had just met at a ball.

'Still good,' he said, nodding to her designs and stretching his legs out in front of him as if sitting was an alien experience. 'What's it for?'

She placed the mugs down on the table, not even thinking to find the coasters she usually insisted upon, and closed the sketchbook.

'I was just passing the time.' She sat down on the chair opposite and crossed one leg over the other.

Dante opened his mouth as if to continue, but as he did so his mobile phone rang. 'I'm sorry—I have to get this.'

He stood then, and turned to look out of her window, speaking rapidly in Italian. As he did so he ran his hand absent-mindedly over the swimming trophy on her windowsill—the one she had dug out on her return from Tuscany, when she had been determined to put a little of herself back in this room. But at this moment in time she felt as if she was barely there at all, for Dante seemed to fill every inch of it.

Faye was still watching the movement of his finger when with his other hand he replaced the slimline mobile in his inside jacket pocket, revealing a flash of deep red lining, and turned to face her. 'I apologise.'

'Don't worry about it,' she said frankly. Business would always come first with him. It was who he was. And if she had remembered that he only respected people who shared his view they wouldn't be here now.

'You needn't feel obliged to come round and check up on me, Dante. You have a business to run; I know you're needed elsewhere.'

'That was actually why I came.'

To discuss business? Faye nodded slowly. 'The interest I owe on your initial advance can be paid direct to your account in Italy at the end of the month, if that is what you mean.' It might mean she missed her first loan repayment to the bank, but that was preferable to being indebted to him.

He looked directly at her then, the hard lines of his face taut with incredulity. 'No, Faye, that is not what I meant. I told you I will gladly invest.'

Why? Because it suited him for her to feel as if she owed him something?

He sat back down on the sofa and continued. 'That call was my office in Rome. These last two days I have been looking for suitable premises for my new head office. In London. The sale is going through as we speak.'

Now it was her turn to stare in disbelief. He was moving? To *London*? Faye felt as if all her worries had just been placed under the microscope and magnified by one hundred. So when he had said they would come to some arrangement he hadn't intended that he would only see their child at high times and holidays. He had genuinely meant they would share. Which meant she would never escape him—that whatever he did, whoever he did it with, would be right under her nose.

'But why?' she asked, truly amazed. Of course it made

logical sense—but when had Dante ever paid attention to that? Would he really change his whole life, leave his beloved Italy and alter the direction of the company he had spent his life building, to take on this role he had never asked for?

He frowned, as if the reason was as obvious as a simple times table. 'I wish my child to be brought up equally, by two parents. That is not feasible if we live in different countries. You wish to live here. I can work anywhere.'

There he was again, turning the situation to suit what he wanted. Faye felt defeated.

'Two parents in the same place, but who are not married,' she whispered, almost to herself, as if to stop her mind imagining otherwise. This conversation seemed so similar to the one they had only nights ago, yet so different.

'It was a mistake to ask you to marry me.'

An expression clouded his eyes that she had never seen before. It was something like remorse, and it didn't sit well on him. But the pity in his voice sat even worse on her. Did he have to spell it out?

'You considered you were doing what was right for this child.' Faye looked down, folding the hem of her jumper into a concertina, her voice such a monotone it was like a phone line gone dead.

'Yes,' he said, and the word had never sounded so laborious as he was forced to admit to himself that in spite of his desperate attempts not to repeat the mistakes his mother had made he had failed anyway. For he had been just as incapable of seeing any point of view other than his own, and in doing so had tried to trap Faye into a marriage that could never have worked.

He stood up suddenly, as if he was eating a date he hadn't

realised contained a stone that needed spitting out. 'But that wasn't the only reason I asked.'

Faye looked up from her mug of coffee, knitting her brows tightly together. Was he attempting to make her feel better? Because whatever game he was playing it just felt as if he was twisting the knife even deeper, and it made her livid.

'What then, Dante? You waltzed into Matteson's fully intending to get down on bended knee before you even knew I was carrying your child, but you just thought you'd set the scene first by demanding more money?' she bit out sarcastically.

'I didn't come because of the damn money.' His charming mouth twisted, as if he had bitten down on that stone by mistake. 'I came because I missed you.'

Faye hardnened her heart against his empty words.

'You missed our affair, you mean?' she asked, expecting his expression to intensify the minute she referred to it so recklessly, and surprised to find it did not. '*That* is why you came? Because you doubted I could repay you any interest on the sum you had lent me, and therefore you intended that I repay you in sexual favours?' Faye forced down the erotic image that popped into her head unbidden. 'I'm sure you can find yourself another willing mistress. If the papers are anything to go by, they're just queuing up to replace me!' Faye drained her coffee cup and banged it down on the table.

'I thought so too, at first,' he admitted, his expression grim. 'But I discovered I didn't want anyone else.'

'Because I am the only woman to have ever ended an affair before you did, perhaps? After all, you had no desire to come after me the *first* time you left my bed.'

He shook his head. She did not know if it was in denial or regret. 'I did you much wrong Faye, I know that. You were an employee in my care, and when I robbed you of your virginity the only way I could justify it to myself was by blaming you— by thinking you were a temptress to whom I had fallen prey.'

'I'm sorry I fell short of your standards.'

'It was my standards that were the problem. It was easier to push you away, to blame you, than it was to admit my own guilt. When I discovered you hadn't taken the dress I knew I had been wrong to judge you by every other woman I had ever known, and I decided to call you. But then I found that you were already abroad with someone else, and I was too jealous to entertain even the idea that it might have been innocent.' He paced uneasily. 'When you returned, begging for money, I had all the evidence I needed and none of the guilt to stop me taking you as my mistress.'

It explained things, of course—made them crystal-clear, in fact. But knowing his motivation, even understanding where it had come from, wasn't easing her pain. It didn't change anything. Their two worlds were still as irreconcilable as they had ever been.

'And what now? You choose to believe the truth because I am carrying your child?'

'A few weeks after you left Tuscany I was at a function in Rome when I ran into Chris.' He looked at her shamefacedly, as if that one sentence was enough. 'He was with his partner.'

'Rick?' Faye asked coolly. 'What about him?' So he had finally worked out that Chris was gay. What did he want? A medal?

'I realised that I might have got things wrong. But then to come to Matteson's and discover you were pregnant and hadn't even told me!'

Faye felt her own anger soften. 'I should have told you.'

She raised hooded eyes to look at him as the severity of her own mistake seeped through her. But Dante was lost in his own thoughts.

'When I thought about why you hadn't told me—though you could have come to me for money, or ensured you were never pregnant at all—I realised it was because you fully intended to raise this child alone. Worse still, I knew you were perfectly capable of making a damn good job of it.'

'You were angry because you thought I'd be a good mother?' Faye asked, bewildered.

'No. I was angry because after you had given yourself to me all those years ago I should have kept you for myself.'

Faye remembered something Elena had said about how possessive he was over the women he cared about, but her head was still spinning.

'I was even angrier at myself two days ago.' The admission was quiet, almost under his breath. 'When you—' His voice had started loudly but now softened, his Italian lilt suddenly prominent. 'When you thought you had lost our baby.' The anguish on his face was like watching something being crushed. 'I knew it was breaking your heart, but you were glad to be free of me. I realised that although I had thought we could make a marriage work, you had only agreed because I gave you no alternative if you wished to see your child. And I hated myself. That is not a pleasant feeling.'

Faye let out a deep sigh. She bet that feeling was an improvement on loving someone blindly for your entire adult life. How much they had both got wrong.

'Do you suppose I only agreed to become your wife because you blackmailed me?'

Dante frowned—the way he always did, she now realised

with affection, when he was forced to confront any perspective other than his own.

'If that is the case, how do you explain why I gave myself to you at eighteen? Or why I barely put up a fight against becoming your mistress?'

Dante began pacing again. 'I may not like to admit it, Faye, but I do know a woman has the same—needs—as a man. Which is precisely why…' he pursed his lips '…it would be wrong of me to marry you and take away your freedom.'

'You think if I do not marry you I will find some other man?'

'I may be a consummate lover, Faye, but I have no doubt that you will find someone else, no.'

She remembered her moment of clarity, which had hit her like the swell of the ocean. Would it be laying her heart too bare to tell him? No, it would be denying she had a heart not to.

'Then for once in your life you underestimate yourself, Dante. You have been my only lover.'

There had not been many moments in Dante's fast-paced life when it had felt as if the world froze for a moment on its axis, but this was one of them. In fact, when he thought about it, he could only recall one other occasion when time had seemed to stop: it had been many years ago, when he had looked up from his menu in a particular restaurant at a particular waitress.

'How is this possible?'

They were the same words he had uttered when he had discovered she was pregnant, Faye noticed. Funny how he was so intelligent in every way she knew except when it came to the things which ought to be blindingly obvious.

'After a rejection like that I wasn't exactly inspired to go looking. Not that anyone ever crossed my path who made me want to,' she said uneasily.

They looked at each other for a long moment before he spoke again, breaking their gaze. 'But like you said, for a marriage to work it requires more than sex.'

She got to her feet then, and reached out to take hold of his fingers gently in her own, making him face her. 'You're right. It does. So why do you suppose I *still* tried to resist becoming your wife—even though Tuscany is where I would most want to bring up our child—even though you told me if I accepted I had no need to worry about Matteson's and that I could continue my designing if I wanted to?'

It was the biggest risk she had ever taken, but suddenly she knew it was time.

'Because I love you, Dante. Because the thought of hiding that every day, as I had to when I was your mistress, tore me apart.'

He raised his eyes to meet hers, and for the first time ever she saw the look of cynicism vanish and the hard lines of his face soften.

'You love me.' He repeated. It was not a question. He was testing the words on his lips, exploring them, revelling in them. It was many years since he had heard them spoken—a lifetime since he had heard them and known that nothing was being asked from him in return. And Faye realised that maybe what had changed most fundamentally of all was Dante himself.

'This means you will reconsider becoming my wife?' His voice was soft, tentative.

'That depends why you are asking me, Mr Valenti,' Faye

teased. A smile was beginning to spread across her lips, and then, as if it was infectious, to Dante's face too.

'You know why, Miss Matteson. Because I think I've loved you since the minute I laid eyes on you,' he said, reaching for her other hand with his. 'And more than anything I want you to be my wife, to have a family with you.'

He had always dreamed of a family sitting down around a dining table. Suddenly, the family had faces: theirs.

'Well…' Faye said, pausing for a painfully long moment, her finger raised to her lips in seductive consideration. 'I think I can agree to your contract.'

'Then you are even more foolish than I thought,' Dante replied, only able to keep his sensuous lower lip from curving into a wicked, self-satisfied grin for a second.

'How so?' Faye tilted her chin at him provocatively.

'Because, *bella*, your lips are not yet upon mine.'

And with that he took her possessively in his arms and kissed her, until they forgot who and where they were—forgot everything except that they belonged to each other.

HARLEQUIN *Presents*

The LEOPARDI BROTHERS

Sicilian by name…scandalous,
scorching and seductive by nature!

CAPTIVE AT THE SICILIAN BILLIONAIRE'S COMMAND
by *Penny Jordan*

Three darkly handsome Leopardi men must hunt down
their missing heir. It is their duty—as Sicilians, as sons,
as brothers! The scandal and seduction they will leave in
their wake is just the beginning….

Book #2811

Available April 2009

Look out for the next two stories in this
fabulous new trilogy from Penny Jordan:

THE SICILIAN BOSS'S MISTRESS in May
THE SICILIAN'S BABY BARGAIN in August

HPI2811

REQUEST YOUR FREE BOOKS!

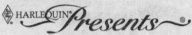

2 FREE NOVELS
PLUS 2
FREE GIFTS!

PASSION GUARANTEED SEDUCTION

YES! Please send me 2 FREE Harlequin Presents® novels and my 2 FREE gifts (gifts are worth about $10). After receiving them, if I don't wish to receive any more books, I can return the shipping statement marked "cancel". If I don't cancel, I will receive 6 brand-new novels every month and be billed just $4.05 per book in the U.S. or $4.74 per book in Canada, plus 25¢ shipping and handling per book and applicable taxes, if any*. That's a savings of close to 15% off the cover price! I understand that accepting the 2 free books and gifts places me under no obligation to buy anything. I can always return a shipment and cancel at any time. Even if I never buy another book, the two free books and gifts are mine to keep forever.

106 HDN ERRW   306 HDN ERRL

Name	(PLEASE PRINT)
Address	Apt. #
City	State/Prov. Zip/Postal Code

Signature (if under 18, a parent or guardian must sign)

Mail to the **Harlequin Reader Service:**
IN U.S.A.: P.O. Box 1867, Buffalo, NY 14240-1867
IN CANADA: P.O. Box 609, Fort Erie, Ontario L2A 5X3

Not valid to current subscribers of Harlequin Presents books.

Want to try two free books from another line?
Call 1-800-873-8635 or visit www.morefreebooks.com.

* Terms and prices subject to change without notice. N.Y. residents add applicable sales tax. Canadian residents will be charged applicable provincial taxes and GST. Offer not valid in Quebec. This offer is limited to one order per household. All orders subject to approval. Credit or debit balances in a customer's account(s) may be offset by any other outstanding balance owed by or to the customer. Please allow 4 to 6 weeks for delivery. Offer available while quantities last.

Your Privacy: Harlequin Books is committed to protecting your privacy. Our Privacy Policy is available online at www.eHarlequin.com or upon request from the Reader Service. From time to time we make our lists of customers available to reputable third parties who may have a product or service of interest to you. If you would prefer we not share your name and address, please check here. ☐

HP08R

EXTRA

UNEXPECTED BABIES
One night, one pregnancy!

These four men may be from all over the world–
Italy, a Desert Kingdom, Britain and Argentina–
but there's one thing they all have in common....

When their mistresses fall pregnant after
one passionate night, an illegitimate heir is
unthinkable. The mothers-to-be will become
convenient wives!

**Look for all of the fabulous stories
available in April:**

Androletti's Mistress #49
by MELANIE MILBURNE

**The Desert King's
Pregnant Bride #50**
by ANNIE WEST

The Pregnancy Secret #51
by MAGGIE COX

The Vásquez Mistress #52
by SARAH MORGAN